AN UMA BLANCHARD COZY MYSTERY

MOJITOS & MURDER

1

Moo and Sizzle is a happenin' place to be right now on this doggone cruise ship, judgin' from the crazy line that goes all the way 'round the corner from it, past the Grand Buffet. The Lido Deck is buzzin' with excited people ready to pig out on all the free cuisine the ship has to offer. As a born-and-bred Cajun, you best believe I know good food. Havin' a healthy appetite is a prerequisite for bein' able to call yourself a true Lose-yannan.

Me bein' the foodie I am, I spent a lot of time in the weeks leadin' up to this trip researchin' all of the restaurants on board extensively, readin' reviews so I didn't have to waste time and calories on any sub-par slop.

That's how I found out about *Moo and Sizzle*. It was the Oshannic Aspire's top-rated food joint with the exception of two sit-down restaurants on a lower deck and the Sparta formal dining room, which I plan to take full advantage of tonight. Now that I'm lookin' at the line, I can see that I wasn't the only one who did my homework. It would appear that this place is not as much of a *hidden* gem as I had initially imagined.

I smell ground beef cookin', and my stomach rumbles. I get in line. Might as well grab a little somethin' to hold me over through the mandatory safety spiel. Plus, I can't be downin' mojitos on an empty stomach. That's a rookie move, and a real Cajun knows better.

I stare out at the New Orleans shoreline from the floatin' mall I'm on, and I try to prepare myself for all the bobbin' it's gon' do in this-here green, saltwater gulf for the next few days.

Ah, the Aspire: a brand new-ish Oshannic-branded cruise vessel. The largest and most pristine of its fleet. This honker is a hundred-and-eighty-thousand gross tons of boat built to hold five thousand people, all their baggage (both literal *and* metaphorical), twenty-seven eateries, three theaters, two lounges, three nightclubs, eleven bars, fourteen shops, a formal dining room, three swimming pools, and a casino.

I take in a deep breath of Gulf air and watch a flock of seagulls hoverin' in the air nearby, waitin' to scavenge thrown leftovers. This day is long overdue. Y'see, I was *s'posed* to sail off on this vessel six months ago on its maiden voyage, but my future son-in-law had to up-and-die on us all, and I was stuck in Killjoy through the entirety of the investigation. By the time I helped track down Carl's killer, my ship -- *this ship* -- was already on its way to Mexico.

I shuffle toward the orderin' window. An adorable Latina woman in a hairnet and apron-covered uniform looks at her register and says, "*Hola*! Welcome to *Moo and Sizzle*. What can I get you?"

"Moo Burger with cheese, *Cher*."

"Sure thing, *mija*. Single or double?"

"Uhhhhh… Double, please. Heck, I'm almost seventy. YOLO, as my grandson says."

"You want that double burger loaded?"

"As loaded as my Smith & Wesson CSX."

She stares at me for a moment, motions toward the other end of the long line with her head, and presses a few buttons. She doesn't seem amused. "Your food'll be down there when it's ready, John Wayne."

I step into the line that she points to behind some middle-aged couple and their little blonde girl, who can't be more than ten, if I had to wager a guess. She has a head full of ringlet curls that could rival Shirley Temple's. Her lips are stained popsicle-red, and it makes her look like a store-brand version of JonBenet Ramsay. She's wearin' a hot pink shirt off one shoulder that says *ALWAYS RIGHT* across the front in white letters. Her baby-pink stretch pants hug her scrawny little chicken legs and tuck down into a pair of light-up sneakers, the soles of which are twinklin' like the rainbow-colored lights of a rave. She's facing the wrong direction, turned around in line just… *starin'* at me.

I point to her parents to silently order her to turn around with my index finger, like I'm stirrin' imaginary gazpacho. She doesn't budge, and her bright blue eyes stare at me, unblinking like one of those kids from the *Village of the Damned* remake starrin' that handsome fella with the butt-clefted chin who was in all those spandex-clad superhero movies.

"Take a Polaroid, kid. It'll last longer," I say, instantly regrettin' it. There's no way a ten-year-old is gonna know what a doggone Polaroid is.

"*Pfft.* Did they even *have* Polaroid cameras back in your day?" she retorts. "Didn't they have to draw you guys on cave walls with *charcoal* to remember what you looked like back then?"

She asks it with way more attitude than someone her size should be allowed to have. She's a surprising ratio of sass per square inch. Tiny and vicious. Suddenly, I miss my mangy little monster, Cocodrie, who is no doubt gettin' us banned for life from another pet boardin' facility.

"'Scuse me?" I say, my fists restin' on my hips.

"Fine. You're excused," she says, folding her arms across her chest.

I reel back, my face probably lookin' like I just smelled a bushel of spoiled oysters. I wonder what she weighs. Even bein' sixty-nine years old with bad knees, she seems light enough that I could hurl her over the railin' of this ship like she's a bag of Mardi Gras beads.

I smile smugly and tap her mother's shoulder. The blonde woman turns, confused.

"'Scuse me. Hi, yes, your daughter here is bein' *rude!* You mind puttin' a *muzzle* on that thing?"

My eyes drift back to the little girl.

In your face, kid.

"She's *not* my daughter," the woman says firmly.

The man beside her looks down at the child, then at me, before finally returning his eyes to the tender beef tips and deliciously-aromatic burger patties sizzlin' behind the glass partition.

The towheaded little girl looks up at me, supremely satisfied. She raises an eyebrow as if her face could say, *Your move,* followed by a choice expletive.

The line inches forward toward the pickup window.

"Can you even chew this stuff with those dentures of yours?" she asks, pointin' to what I assume is my double cheeseburger bein' assembled behind the glass.

For a moment, I don't know what to say. *I'm* normally the most unfiltered person for three square miles. Now, I feel like I've been bested by someone barely outta the womb. I decide it's best to ignore her, and I glance around for any sign of Cosmo, my son, or my grand-spawn. None appears to be nearby. I imagine they're all still unpackin' in their staterooms.

"What did you get?" the little girl asks. When I don't answer, she howls, "Uh, hellooooooo?"

Reluctantly, I peer down at her. "You talkin' to me?"

"Yes, Robert De Niro."

I stare at her, stunned.

How the…?

"Ugh. It's from *Taxi Driver*." She lets out a tiny, exasperated sigh. "You know, the film starring a young Jodie Foster long before *The Silence of the Lambs*?"

"I know what *Taxi Driver* is, you little shrimp. I'm just surprised that *you* know what *Taxi Driver* is. Or *Silence of the Lambs*, for that matter!" I stare at her with narrowed eyes. "How *old* are you?"

"Eleven."

Seems like a lie. I was gonna guess nine. "You're a *small* eleven."

"Yeah? Well, you're a *large* one-hundred-and-nine."

"I'm still in my *sixties*, kid." *Well, for about nine more days, that is.*

"Mmm-hmm. Sure." Then, she giggles. It is an absolutely horrid sound, one that a tickled woodpecker might make. "Riiiiiight."

"Don't dodge my question. How do you know what those movies are?"

"I watch what I want. Mom's loaded. She gets me all the streaming channels."

"You can't just roam around all free-range like that at eleven."

"Do you *see* my mother anywhere?" She motions to the people all around us, surging in single-file lines like platelets pulsin' through cholesterol-encrusted veins. "No. And you probably *won't* either. She's probably already three martinis deep, tying one on at the piano bar."

"And where is good ol' *dad*?"

"Ha!" A laugh burbles out of her. "Good one. Rumor has it he's somewhere in Sri Lanka eating tandoori chicken and 'finding himself.'" She uses air quotes with her tiny fingers. "Or at least he *was* last time she heard from him, which was somewhere around four years ago."

"Ah, I see. So you're just allowed to run around all feral like this?"

"There's a term for it, I think."

"*Rabid*?"

"Hatch-key kid, or something like that."

"Latch-key," I correct her, though I don't know *why* I'm even still talkin' to her!

The line wafts forward another three feet or so, and the couple in front of the girl smiles as they receive their plastic cafeteria tray full of sizzlin', made-to-order fare. My stomach grumbles as they walk away with it.

Next, the workers slide the rude child a tray, one with six hot dogs and a small side of fries. She can barely lift it with her skinny, little toothpick arms. She steps away from the counter, hoists one edge onto her shoulder, and stares at me.

And just *keeps* staring...

"Uh, you got a problem, kid?"

"Nope!" she says confidently.

For about thirty seconds, I stand awkwardly, waiting for my meal as her eyes burn holes into me like belly-high laser beams. During this time, she doesn't say a single word.

Finally, they hand me my burger. I take my tray and flash a curt smile at the girl as I walk away in search of an available table on the already crowded lido deck. I spot an empty one across the way and shuffle over to it. I set my tray down and settle into the cushioned seat, feelin' the crunch of cartilage rattle through my knees as I relieve them of their cumbersome burden.

It isn't a moment later that the kid, *this tiny burr in my metaphorical sock,* sets her tray full of a bazillion dogs down on my table and hops up into the upholstered chair across from me.

"Um, *excuse* me?"

"Why? Did you fart?" she asks, then she rips into one of her hot dogs with her teeth. She doesn't even put any ketchup on it, the *monster.* She just eats it plain, like a friggin' sadist.

"What? No," I say, which is a lie. I actually crop-dusted a few little squeakers along my path to the table. The lido deck is wide open, and I knew the wind whippin' through the Gulf would take it all far away, fast. Poor kid was draftin' on me, right in the danger zone. I don't feel bad about it, though. I'm on a fistful of daily fiber pills for my cholesterol, and no one told the little runt to follow me like a towed boat.

"I meant, why are you *sittin' here*, shrimp? I don't remember inviting you."

She shrugs. "Huh. Weird. Well, I guess that's dementia for ya."

"Hey… Make like the doggone little *wasp* you are and buzz off! Go on. Go pester someone else."

"Nah, I'm good." She crams another half a hot dog into her tiny mouth and gnashes the wad of bread and nitrate.

I look around, my eyes doing another scan for Cosmo. And, I s'ppose my family, too.

"They aren't coming," the kid says, finally tearing off the corner of a ketchup packet. Over her fries, she violently extrudes the red contents through the too-small hole. Losing patience, she wrenches the packet, and the remainder comes out in a small explosion like a scaled-down version of the special effects in *Platoon*.

"*Who* isn't coming?"

"Whoever you're looking for right now."

"I'm not lookin' for no one," I lie again, hopin' to see Cosmo's entrancing eyes pierce me through the crowd of hungry vacationers and save me from this conversation.

"Anyone," she corrects. "'Not lookin' for no one' is a double negative."

"You're really gettin' on my doggone nerves, chile."

"Hey, I just call it as I see it." She jams a fry in her mouth and looks up at me. "I know abandonment and desperation when I see it. I'm a latch-key kid, remember?"

I stare at her in horror for a moment. "What *are* you?"

"I'm a fifth-grader." She bobbles her head. "Well, about to be seventh when school starts again, though. They want me to skip a grade. They say I'm too smart to waste my time in sixth."

"You don't say." I roll my eyes and take a bite of my burger. My lids flutter. It's juicy as all get-out and the patties are cooked to perfection, not underdone and not as chewy as the sole of an orthopedic shoe insert, either. The lettuce is crisp, and the onions are sliced to the perfect width. Now I can see why the place has garnered such rave reviews.

"I'm Dolly, by the way."

"I didn't ask," I say before takin' another bite.

"Well, that's my nickname," she continues as if I said nothing at all. "My *real* name is Dorothy. Dorothy Haus. But no one calls me that." She gobbles down another hot dog like she's half piranha.

I chuckle. "Your last name is *Haus*?"

"Yes." Her eyes don't break away from the Jackson Pollock-esque masterpiece of pureed tomato and sugar on the wax paper in front of her. "I'm of German descent."

"That explains *so* much," I mutter as I take another big bite of my food. "So… let me get this straight. You go by *Dolly*."

"I didn't stutter."

"Dolly… Haus?" I jiggle with laughter.

"Yep."

"Like *doll house*?" I'm laughin' so hard now that I might pee. Just a little.

"Wowwwww, are *you* the eleven-year-old, or am I?" She shakes her head. "No wonder everyone you're with ditched you."

Now, I'm irritated. The *underwear* I'm wearin' is older than this twerp, and she thinks she can talk to me like she's Dr. Laura or somethin'?

"Listen, you little prepubescent punk, you need to chill with the attitude."

"I'll do what I please." The kid takes a napkin and gives her ketchup-smeared face an exaggerated wipe before slamming it dramatically down into the puddled remnants of her condiment. She forces a smug smile. "So? What're we doing tonight after the mandatory thing at the Mustard Station?"

"We? *We* aren't doing anything, Dollhouse. *I* will be goin' to the Sparta for the formal dinner and then shuttin' karaoke down. I have no clue what *you're* gon' do."

"Why would you shut karaoke down? What do you have against karaoke?"

"What? Nothin'! I adore karaoke. It's a common expression, child. To shut something down means to stay 'til somethin's closed."

"I think my mom shuts the bar down on the weekends," she volunteers.

"Color me shocked." Then, I cock my head like one of Cosmos' Cavalier King Charles spaniels. "And it's *Muster* Station. Not *Mustard* Station."

She shrugs and jams another dog in her gullet. I watch her eat, a truly grotesque sight. I feel like I'm watching a hungry cheetah tear into a baby gazelle in some kind of nature documentary.

After a pause, she says, "What're you going to sing at karaoke?"

"Yeah, right. Like I'm gonna tell you so you can steal my songs. Nice try." I ignore her, hoping eventually she will take a hint and go away. In glorious silence, I polish off the last bit of my burger and steal a few of the fries off Dolly's tray. Still chewin', I rise from my seat with a pained grunt. "Well, Dollhouse, it's been real."

"Yeah. Real *lame*." There is visible disappointment on her face now. She looks like a ticked-off American Girl doll.

"Ahhh, such *sparkling* wit," I mutter sarcastically. "Enjoy your vacation, kid."

"See you around." The look she gives me is two parts sincere, one part threat.

"*Hopefully not,*" I mutter to myself as I walk away.

2

Day 1 - 5:15 pm
Lifeboat Muster Station
Gulf Deck 4

"Hello, everyone! I'm Cooper Nagilnick. I will be your Funtivities Director on this *beautiful* new boat in our fleet, the Aspire. I'll be leading you in many of your fun-in-the-sun activities for the duration of your cruise," Cooper's voice booms, loud and with gobs of faux enthusiasm. He looks like a real-life hobbit from a Tolkien book with his doughy rectangular body, burnt umber head of curls, and thick, mustache-less beard that makes him look strangely Amish. He keeps pulling up his pants absentmindedly because his rear-end is so flat it's almost concave. There's literally nothing protrudin' enough for his doggone belt to catch on.

He smiles out at the crowd of us, all lined up on the long, narrow path in front of the hangin' life boats. "I see you've all found your individual Muster Station. Congratulations! Round of applause! You passed your first and *only* test. That is, unless you decide to sign up for one of our trivia game shows in the Poseidon Theater!"

Behind him, a handful of other crew members stand, each smiling. They're all dressed in matchin' uniforms with teal embroidery over their left breasts featuring the ship's logo. Their pants are bleached whiter'n Denzel Washington's teeth and look about as crisp as a fresh, Cajun *groton.*

"Before we can disembark from the dock, we must go over a few safety tips for using the emergency lifeboats. I know, I know. BOR-ING!" He laughs like he just told a joke, even though he didn't. I think he knows most of us who've cruised before ignore this spiel just like the safety mumbo-jumbo before takeoff on a Delta flight.

Yada, yada, seatbelts. Yada, yada, your seat is a flotation device. Yada, yada, put your own doggone mask on before you worry about any of the little crotch goblins running around.

We get it. If there really *was* an emergency -- like if we slammed into an iceberg like they did in that DiCaprio flick -- none of us are gon' remember this crud in panic mode anyhow.

Through the crowd, I see Cosmo wave at me. Beside him stands his daughter, Isa, as well as my son, Daniel, Daniel's wife, Jane, Stokely, and Duncan — aka my grand-spawn. I think thin thoughts and squeeze behind the rows of people to approach, picturin' myself floatin' through unnoticed with the grace of some waifish specter even though, in reality, my little bit of belly chub and low-hangin' boobs are brushin' up against the backs of at least *half* these sweaty strangers.

When the crowd finally spits me out, Cosmo points to the vacant space he just made right next to him, like he wants me to join. I oblige, tryin' to hide my smile as my cheeks blush. Despite the cool Gulf 'a Mexico breeze blowin' over the rails from the ripplin' water, I can still feel the heat radiatin' off of my handsome neighbor like someone's a cranked-up propane heater nearby. Almost feels like a hot flash. He's lookin' mighty fine, and I have the sudden desire to wrap myself around him like that snake on the Red Cross logo.

Alas, I decide, instead, to behave myself.

Duncan and Stokely point to an infant a few rows ahead. Stokely mimes that he wants to drop-kick it over the side of the boat. Then, while laughing, Duncan flicks his brother so hard in the side of his head that the sound of the thump rings out and people all around us turn to look. Jane offers an almost silent apology to the agitated adults, her weary eyes beggin' for their mercy.

There's somethin' wrong with those kids, I tell ya.

Nagilnick drones on about how the lifeboats, which are currently danglin' just high enough to avoid bein' slapped like Farrah Fawcett's character in *The Burning Bed* by the punishing seas. I zone out, catchin' a whiff of

Cosmo's cologne mixed with briny ocean air, and it dawns on me that I'm *finally* on vacation. My almost-son-in-law thwarted my last attempt to board this cruise, but now I realize I made it and it's time for a little well-earned relaxation.

The moment this thought enters my head, I feel tense again because through the crowd, I see Dolly starin' at me from a vase-shaped hole between the two pear-shaped adult butts in front of her, neither of which is her mother, I'm sure. Her eyes glare at me from the height of one of the women's fanny packs and she offers a friendly wave with her little hand. I look away. With Duncan and Stokely here, there's already *way* more children than I'd consider *ideal* for a relaxin' getaway.

When I finally glance back to see if she is still starin', Dolly has vanished like a ghost, slinkin' back behind the *derrieres* of more adults.

Cooper claps his hands together once, hard. "I'd like to also announce that aboard this vessel are the gold, silver, and bronze winners of this year's Texas Hot Dog Eating Championship. Let's give these folks a round of applause!"

An enthusiastic clap sounds among the group, and one older man releases an ear-piercin' whistle as three portly men with matchin' *Relish the Day* shirts silently thank everyone for the applause.

"If you'd like to go dog-for-dog with your fellow cruisers, these reigning champs will be the judges in Sunday's hot dog eating contest at the *You're the Wurst*

Grille. Make sure you sign up at the kiosk by the Minnow Pool on the Lido Deck!"

"Dad!" Duncan exclaims, tuggin' on Daniel's polo. "I wanna sign up for the hot dog eating competition!"

Daniel shakes his head. "Absolutely not. Those things are nitrate city."

"What's a nitrate?" Stokely asks.

"It's a preservative people put in meat sometimes," Daniel says.

Then, Duncan flashes an evil grin. "Isn't it an explosive?"

"Well… not the way they do it in hot dogs."

"Oh," Duncan replies, sad, as if his spontaneous idea to make a makeshift incendiary device on the ship was just thwarted. Then, his eyes return to his father. "Are we in Cozumel yet?"

Daniel laughs. "Dunky, we're still in Nawlins. We haven't even left the dock yet."

Duncan growls angrily, tries to punch the air, and accidentally whacks some middle-aged guy in pleated shorts right in the side of the man's bare thigh. He whips around, and Duncan just glares at him. My son apologizes on his behalf.

Finally, Cooper ends our suffering with a loud, "Thank you all for attending, and once again, welcome aboard the Oshannic Aspire!" Nagilnick takes an awkward bow as people cheer. He tugs his droopin' uniform pants up over his non-existent butt and waves, releasin' us all from this hellish limbo. As the crowd disperses, a few people stay to gush over the competitive eaters, each takin' selfies like they're celebrities or somethin', all three in matching baseball-lookin' uniforms with a seventies-style font splashed across big stitched-on hot dogs.

I scoff and nudge Cosmo with an elbow. "Pfft. Can you believe that's even considered a sport, *Cher*? Who'd have thought crammin' your maw with enough preservatives to kill a friggin' Clydesdale'd be somethin' random strangers would *cheer* for?"

"I don't understand the whole competitive eating thing, but, then again, I've had to stay in shape for a while now. You jus' never know in my industry. I could wake up one day and find out I'm doin' helicopter jumps in a tux for the next Bond film in a month."

"What a life you must lead," I swoon, starin' at biceps bulgin' out the sleeves of his palm frond-patterned Hawaiian shirt. Muscles so hard you could thin-slice an andouille sausage on 'em like a bamboo cuttin' board.

"Whatcha up to now?" I ask, snappin' myself out of my brief, smitten trance.

"Oh, I imagine I'll poke around the boat a bit. See how long the line for shuffleboard is."

"Want a mojito?" I ask. "I'm buyin'. I got one'a those all-you-can-drink passes."

He smirks, and my already-weakened knees feel like they could buckle at the sight of those ice-blue eyes. "I bought it, too. With what we Cajuns can knock back, it just made the most fiscal sense, you know?"

His smile widens, and I subtly grab the chrome guardrail behind me so I don't collapse at the sight of it. My God, he makes me as hot and stirred-up inside as a good bowl of gumbo!

"What about you? Where're you off to, Uma Mae?"

My name -- ugly as it is -- sounds like each letter has been dipped in sugar like a praline when it comes from his mouth.

"I think I'm gonna go do a little walkin', see where everything's at, burn off a few calories before formal dinin' tonight. You gon' be there?"

"I was debating a burger, but Isa really wants me to get gussied up, so we'll see. I don't usually wear a suit unless it's for a role. I'm more of a jeans and cowboy boots kinda fella, you know?"

Oh, I know. I could paint that normally Levi-clad butt from memory.

"Well, I hope to see you there," I say, tryin' to play it cool.

"Yeah, maybe."

"You gon' come see me karaoke tonight?"

"I'm sure gonna try."

"I take requests." I grin slyly.

"I heard your version of 'Pour Some Sugar On Me' is absolutely legendary."

"Yeah, there's some video of it floatin' around somewhere on the social medias," I say proudly, tryin' not to sound *too* braggadocios. "That the one you want me to sing for ya?"

He chuckles quietly. "Not much of a Def Leppard fan, myself. Lemme think on it. I'm sure I can think up a doozy."

"You do that." I laugh. "But it's gotta be rock. And it's gotta be the good stuff. Seventies or eighties, preferably. None'a this modern crud."

"Noted. Catch you later, Uma Mae." He smiles again and turns to walk away.

That's when I see her again, *Dollhouse* with the blonde ringlet curls, starin' at me from just a few feet away.

She nods to acknowledge me. "You said you're takin' requests?"

I laugh.

Then, I laugh a little harder.

"Not from you."

"Dang. I figured you'd get up there and hum the theme song to Jurassic Park or something since you're a dinosaur."

With that, I leave in a huff.

3

Day 1 - 7:13 pm
Sparta Formal Dining Lounge
Lobby Deck 3

I glitter like a disco ball as I approach the hostess station. I tell the woman my room number, and she hands me a menu. A well-dressed man with the hint of a French-tinged African accent whisks me through a huge room of well-dressed people to a large U-shaped booth near the back. I see quite a few familiar faces already seated there.

"Mee-Maw, where were you?!" Duncan growls rudely, his face shoved into the palm of one hand like he's been waiting for a decade. "You're late!"

"Oh, please, Dunky, lay off, would ya? When *you* have to cram your body into ten yards 'a Spanx just to fit into a sequin gown, then we'll talk tardiness. I nearly fell squeezin' in these doggone things, and I heard some kinda weird pop in my left knee. Snapped like a dry branch when

I finally got it through one of the crotch holes. Thought I did some kinda permanent damage. Turns out, I'm just old, thank God."

"Uma, what on earth are you wearing?" Jane asks in her barely-audible voice. It always annoys me how quietly she talks. My hearin' ain't the greatest, and the closer I lean in to hear her, the quieter she always gets. I've grown accustomed to just smilin' and noddin' whenever she talks in my direction, followed by the occasional, cleverly-flexible reply of, '*You don't say!*'

Lord only knows what I've accidentally agreed to over the years.

I look down at my dress, a long gown drenched in primary-colored sequins in a swirl pattern of vibrant reds, oranges, and blues. It's wild and stands out. You can see me comin' from a mile away. It's gonna look incredible under the par-cans of the karaoke lounge when I'm in the spotlight tonight.

"You like it? I got it at Geautreaux's last week. Treated myself."

"Ma, you look like a macaw." Daniel's eyes dart away like he's embarrassed.

"What's a macaw?" Duncan asks.

"*A parrot,*" Jane says in her whisper of a voice.

Stokely breaks out into a giggle that sounds like a cartoon chipmunk. "Oh yeah. She really *does* look like a macaw."

"Well, I think you look *lovely,* Uma Mae," Cosmo's daughter, Isa, says, liftin' her champagne flute as if to toast me.

"I second that," Cosmo offers quietly with a hint of a smile. I could swear he winks as he lifts a stubby crystal glass of whiskey to his lips.

"Thank you, dear." Then, I glare at Daniel. "See? At least *someone* has taste 'round here."

"You just look a little overdressed. That's all. You didn't have to get all dolled-up like you were goin' to the Oscars," Daniel says. "They said 'cruise elegant' or 'smart casual,' not 'red carpet formal.'"

"It's formal night! What the heck is the point of keepin' all my fancy dresses if I never get to wear 'em?" I caw.

"Maybe you *should* sell them," Stokely chimes in, gnawing on the tines of his gold salad fork like it's coated in Godiva chocolate.

Then, Duncan smarts off, too. "Stoke, who the heck is gonna buy *that* thing?" He looks at me. "You should just burn it, Mee-Maw."

"Thanks."

"Actually," he says like he's had an epiphany, "you should let *us* burn it!"

"No! No burning anything," Daniel growls, then does a slow blink up at the chandelier that says *Dear Jesus, give me strength.* He rubs his temples like the twins are givin' him a migraine.

"That's it? That's *all* you're gon' say to them when they're back-talkin' their elder like that?" I grumble.

"Oh, allow me," a dark-haired young man between the only two empty seats says as he slides his padded crimson chair out. His foot catches on something, and he nearly topples back into the seated fella behind him, regainin' his composure just before disastrously dumpin' his drink on the unsuspectin' diner.

He sloshes a little of the drink in his hand at me. "Friggin' boat is all *over* the place," he says, slurrin' a little, as if *that* is the reason for his stumblin' around and not the glass of vodka-soda in his hand. I can tell from his lack of a southern accent and his inability to consume an inhuman amount of liquor that he *ain't* from Louisiana.

He pulls out my chair and then theatrically motions for me to sit as if he's a paid driver hired to escort me into my limo. He looks like he's in his twenties, barely old enough to drink.

"Thank you." I nod at him as I take my seat, gruntin' as I lower into the chair.

Daniel points at the strangers at the other end of the oval table, his hand cuttin' through the air like an ax. "While we were waitin' on you, we were all just getting acquainted. Ma, this is Alan and Marisol."

He points to the two old fogies on the end — and by *that*, I mean *substantially* older'n me. They're dressed in muted, borin' tones like they just got released from a church service that condemns colorful fabrics like it's some long-lost law in Leviticus. Marisol doesn't make eye contact with anyone. She just shields her brows with one hand and waves like the last swipe of a dyin' windshield wiper with the other.

"Pleasure," I lie, forcin' a smile, feelin' my eyes wrinkle like old tissue paper in the corners. "Uma Blanchard."

Daniel's hand chops through the air again at the drunk kid beside me. "And this is… I'm sorry. I have already forgotten your name. My apologies."

The sloshed man hoists what's left of his drink. "Dev-in. Like Kevin."

"That's right," my son mutters.

"Devin Cohelo, ma'am. Nice to meet you." Devin smiles so hard his eyes disappear, buried behind little crescent moon slits of dark lashes.

"You old enough to be drinkin' that, boy?" I flash him a hint of a smile.

He grins back. "Yes, ma'am, I am."

"Good." I bob my head at him and look at my menu. I'm starvin' again, and everythin' sounds so good. Chilled shrimp cocktail, spicy corn chowder, hot crawfish fettuccine, beef carpaccio… and, heck, those are just the starters!

A slender blonde approaches, dressed in a pressed-and-starched uniform donning the teal Aspire logo. She smiles at me, her eyes a little alarming, like she's bein' held at gunpoint. Her smile screams *duress*.

"Good evening, ma'am. My name is Alena. I'll be your waitress here in the formal dining room. Can I get you something to drink?"

"Yeah, I'll have a mojito, extra mint, extra lime. Top shelf rum." I point to her. "I'll be able to *tell* the difference."

"Yes, ma'am." She nods as I flash her my alcohol pass. It allows me one alcoholic drink on the house every hour. My hour should be up in about 60 seconds. I timed it out just so. It's why I took my sweet time gettin' here.

"Keep 'em comin'. And," I look around the table and slap the folds of my fancy menu closed, air *whooshing* the fabric napkin beside me like a stiff breeze, "I'm ready to order if y'all are."

"You sure? You barely looked at the menu," Jane asks in another barely audible whisper.

"Jane, you know me better'n that. I'm a retiree and a foodie. What in God's good name makes you think I didn't do my homework? I knew what I's gon' eat on this boat before I even stepped foot on that gangway this afternoon."

"I should've known." Jane nods and looks at her own menu for a moment before closin' it.

Daniel shakes his head. "You probably already scoped out everywhere you wanna go at the ports, too."

"Yeah, pretty much. Food-wise, at least." I look at Alena and smile. "Alright, *Cher*, I s'pose I'll go first. For my starter, I'll have the crawfish fettuccine. Main course, I'll have the grilled jumbo bacon-wrapped shrimp. See if the chef can sprinkle a little Tony's seasonin' on those bad boys, if they got it. And for dessert, gimme the panna cotta, would ya?"

Alena scribbles rapidly and smiles before takin' the orders of all my tablemates. I look around and take in my surroundings. The Sparta Formal Dining Lounge is a two-story themed space with wide, sweepin' panorama windows offering a view of a honey-and-magenta sunset bloomin' over a flat horizon of dark Gulf waters. A massive oval chandelier hangs over the open center of the room, studded with warm light bulbs on its exterior, crystals danglin' like long icicles all through the middle. Statues of muscular Spartan warriors stand rigid between some of the windows, each wearin' a gleaming helmet, ready for war, a spear gripped in their dominant hands.

The cinnamon-brown carpet is so short, I imagine it is only used to dampen the sound of all the chatter comin' from the well-dressed diners in each of the tufted chairs. Gold floor-to-ceiling poles wrapped in faux ivy pepper the room, most likely there for structural integrity. Over the entrance sits a huge paintin', a banner over two fake, life-size olive trees illustratin' the Battle of Thermopylae against the Persians.

As Alena takes off toward the kitchen, Cosmo unfurls his napkin and smooths it over his lap. "Uma, have you figured out what you're gonna sing tonight?"

"I thought you'd never ask," I joke with a smile. "I'm still narrowin' it down."

"Please, God, say you're not doing 'Pour Some Sugar on Me' again, Ma," Daniel says.

"I'm thinkin' of starting the vay-cay out with some B52's or some Bachman Turner. Maybe sprinkle in a little Meatloaf. But, I do take requests." I bat my eyes at him expectantly.

"As long as it's not that God-awful Nickelback again."

"You just hate Nickelback 'cause it's fun to join in on the jokes. If your friends all jumped off a bridge, would you jump off, too?" I snarl.

"If you sing that one where Kroger talks about liking the girl's pants around her knees again, I *would*, actually, yes. I'd toss myself off the bow tonight, in fact. Bet," Daniel says. "Or, God forbid, if I had to sit through that Elton John one you butchered again." He makes a sour face.

"Hey!" I wag a finger angrily at him. "I may have bombed the first half of that one, but I totally saved it with the air-harmonica. Ask anyone who was there. I got a standin' ovation!"

"They were humoring you because you're a million years old and still doing karaoke, Ma. No one thinks your air-instruments are actually funny."

"One thousand percent disagree," I grumble, starin' at my scarlet plate charger feelin' a bomb of blindin' white-hot anger explode across my heavily-made-up face.

"Mee-Maw, you should do 'Mr. Roboto' again," Duncan says with a giggle.

"Nah, I almost threw my hip out last time doin' the robot," I say.

"No, that was the Ricky Martin song," Stokely chimes in.

"I thought you needed an ambulance that night," Daniel mutters, polishin' his fork. "I thought you were *havin'-a-major-stroke-ah.*"

Jane snickers and then covers her lips so as not to irk me. An apologetic look flits across her features.

"What do you wanna hear me sing?" I ask my grandchildren.

"Oh, we won't be there. We're playing mini golf tonight," Stokely says.

I look at Jane, my face fraught with worry. "You're gonna give them weapons? Made of metal? There's gon' be civilian casualties, I tell ya."

Jane frowns. "We'll be right there with them, Uma. They're not gonna assault anybody." She looks at her kids. "Are you?"

They just snicker.

"So… They're hosting karaoke somewhere tonight?" Devin, the drunk, clumsy guy, asks as if his brain is on a two-minute delay, crushin' one of the ice cubes from his drink between his molars like Cocodrie does.

Or *did*. Back when he had doggone *teeth*.

"Sure are. The cruise app says they're hostin' it all four nights. It starts in the Hammerhead Lounge at nine," I reply.

"That means she'll be there at eight fifty-nine waitin' at the door," my son says to Devin.

I chuckle. He's not wrong. I turn to Devin. "You should come. See me shine."

"It is *truly* unforgettable when Uma takes the stage," Jane mumbles quietly to him, but the way she says it, it doesn't exactly sound like a compliment.

"You know any duets or harmonies on any? I'll sing with you," Devin says, liftin' his glass to his mouth again with a smirk. Three of his fingers have bandages on 'em, each one lookin' like it came out of a different box of Band-Aids. They don't all appear to be from the same injury. I'd bet a fresh king cake that his trippin' wasn't a one-off. Kid seems like he's probably clumsy even when he ain't drunk.

"Oh, Lord, don't encourage her," Daniel says to him. "Whole family is still traumatized from the time she performed 'Baby Got Back' by Sir-Mix-A-Lot, complete with dance moves."

"I slayed that night, Daniel." I fold my arms across my chest.

Daniel scoffs. Cosmo doesn't say a word, but he flashes my boy a look that screams, *Hey, respect your elders*. It makes me smile when I see him do it. Cosmo's blue eyes lock on mine for a moment before drifting over to the short skirt-thingy of the Spartan statue nearest our table.

"I'll sing backup on whatever you want, kid. I welcome any extra time on the stage," I say to Devin. "If it's from the seventies or eighties, don't worry, I already know the words, too."

I look at Cosmo. "You and Isa gon' join us?"

"Maybe tomorrow night," Isa says with a flat smile. "Dad promised we could go hit the roulette table at the casino like old times."

"I took her to L'Auberge when she turned twenty-one, and we stayed up all night playin' red numbers. At the start of the night, I had given her two hundred to play with. When we finally drove home in the mornin', it was light out, and she had about four grand in her pocket." Cosmo pats the back of his daughter's hand softly. "Kinda been a tradition in the twenty years since, any time we're near a casino."

"Aw, that's sweet. Well, I hope you win loads of cash tonight," I say, a little sad that Cosmo isn't gonna be there.

Fortunately, we have four more days together on this floating mall. I'm sure we'll get into *plenty* of shenanigans in that time.

4

The colored lights from the par-cans are spinnin' wild when I wiggle my way through the throng of people toward the songbooks. My parrot-colored sequins refract light in every direction as I make my way over to snatch one of the coveted binders. I take it to an empty leather booth and flip it open, lookin' through their selection to see if any of my favorites jump off the page. I see someone approach and then fall up the carpeted steps toward me, sendin' his glass — and its contents — flyin'.

Devin Cohelo.

Biggest klutz I've maybe ever seen.

Devin picks himself up. A cocktail waitress grabs his glass off the floor as he dusts himself off. I overhear her ask if he's okay, and he responds simply by orderin' a double of whiskey, neat. Probably so he doesn't accidentally choke to death on an ice cube, at this rate.

"Well! Fancy seeing you here." His attempt at a joke falls flat. I literally jus' told him I'd be here. "This seat taken?" He points to the empty chunk of booth to my right.

The lounge is decorated with gaudy marine cut-outs, silhouettes of various sharks and aquatic creatures backlit by several hues of aquamarine and navy blue all around the ceiling. Each metal protrusion hangs like an odd-shaped guillotine blade overhead.

A man in his twenties, barely older'n Devin, waltzes out to the microphone stand on the stage and unclips it. He runs a hand through his short, black hair and looks out at the audience. With zero stage presence whatsoever, he flatly says, "Welcome to Hammerhead Karaoke. I'm Lawrence Fordham, your host. The sign-up sheet is over here at my booth near the songbooks. If you'd like to sing, make sure you come over and see me."

He clips the mic back into the stand and walks back out to his booth, doin' a little hop over one of the microphone cords. Once he plops into his seat, out comes his cell phone to occupy all of his attention. He leans back, holds the cell sideways, snaps a photo of himself, and goes back to typin' something on it.

"What are we duettin'? 'Paradise By the Dashboard Lights?' 'Love Shack?'" I ask Devin, my killer solo selection already chosen. I just wish I had my fluffy, crimped Dee Schneider blonde wig with me.

Devin stares up at the metal sharks on the ceiling, a poignant expression on his youthful face. "I don't know either of those very well. These are the ones I'm thinking of. Tell me if you think you could sing backup or harmony on any."

"Hit me with your best shot."

"I don't know that one very well, either."

"Devin, I wasn't suggestin' we sing Pat Benatar. I was just tellin' you to spit out the names of the songs." I raise an eyebrow and try to focus on the same nurse shark cutout that he is. "Although, I do a *mean* 'Hell is for Children.'"

Just then, Dolly slides into the vacant part of the booth on my right.

"What are we singing tonight?" she asks.

"Speaking of 'Hell is for Children.'" I roll my eyes and look at the kid. "*We* ain't singin' squat, kid. Now beat it."

"Cher?" she asks, ignorin' my demand completely. "You look like the kinda old fart who'd whip out a Sonny and Cher song like 'I Got You, Babe.'"

"First of all, I do Cher better than *Cher* does Cher, okay, twerp? But I don't do none of that old stuff. I do, like, 'Believe' or 'If I Could Turn Back Time.'"

"Yeah, I could see your old vocal cords being able to warble like that," Dolly says matter-of-factly as she riffles through the pages of my songbook.

"They don't have much of whatever nonsense you kids are listenin' to these days."

"Oh? And what exactly are kids *my* age listening to these days?" she asks smugly, callin' me out.

"The Baby Shark song."

Dolly howls with sarcastic laughter. "I'm eleven, not three."

"I guarantee you're a Swifty. I can see it in your beady little eyes, you swamp rat."

Dolly chuckles loudly with more hammy over-dramatics than a junior high improv class. She goes limp in her seat, slidin' half beneath the table. Suddenly, she snaps out of the laugh and shoots up until her posture is perfection. "Good try, oldie-locks. Not my style."

"Oh yeah? Enlighten me, then."

She starts countin' things off on her tiny fingers, each one not even the width of a sugary pirouette. "Try *the Animals.*"

I bark out a laugh. Surely, she can't be serious. "As in the animals on Sesame Street?"

She rolls her eyes and counts one off on her extended middle finger, an exaggerated and extremely *rude* gesture for an eleven-year-old. "Supertramp. James Taylor. ELO. You want me to go on?"

Dear lord, she's like a tiny version of *me*, musically.

"You can't even spell ELO," I say suspiciously. The comment confuses her, and then I realize what I said made no sense. She has me all flustered!

"I think I'll do an ELO song," she says, flippin' through the plastic-covered pages with a haughty expression.

"Ha! That'll be the day."

She cocks a small blonde brow at me. "The vinyl LP collection at my house is fire." She waves me away dismissively. "Eh, you probably don't even know what an LP is. You probably listen to big band era songs on AM radio or something."

I turn to Devin, flabbergasted. "The nerve on this girl! She's barely older'n my pantyhose, and she's giving me a lecture on LPs?"

"What's an LP?" Devin asks, sincerely.

Dolly and I both just stare at him.

"What? I got XM." He says it as if it's an excuse to not know what physical media is.

"Tell you what," Dolly says as she slams the book closed. "If I do 'Don't Bring Me Down' and don't miss a beat, you gotta sign up to do the hot dog eating contest with me."

"There's no way you're doin' that song without missin' a beat, *Cher*. And there's *no* way I'm fillin' up on cylindrical lips-and-buttholes when there are five-star Michelin-rated chefs on board. Plus, do you know what my primary care physician would say?"

"Chicken," Dolly says, shovin' the song book at me and climbin' out of the booth. She mimics cryin', like a tiny bully. "Oh, poor me. I'm afraid of what my doctors would say."

"Sign up for the contest yourself."

"They won't let me! They say I need the signature of a parent or guardian."

"Get your mom to do it," I growl.

This comment hurts her. I can see it all over her face. It stuns her to silence. For a split second, I feel guilty enough to say, "Fine. You've got a deal. It's not like you're gonna sing it without messin' it up, anyway." I turn to Devin. "Hit me with your selects, kid."

"Okay, I'm thinking of any of the following…" his dark eyes start to well with tears as he stares up at the ceiling again. "'Red Right Hand.'"

"The Nick Cave song?"

He nods solemnly. "'Sympathy For the Devil' by the Rolling Stones. Or 'In the Air Tonight.'"

"Genesis?" I ask, my face screwed-up like I just smelled a fart.

I'm sensin' a pattern here…

"Phil Collins," Dolly corrects me, shakin' her head like she's in the company of an idiot. "It's from his solo album, you *dunce*."

My brain feels like it is gonna explode. How in the world is an eleven-year-old bestin' me on songs that're thirty years older'n she is?

I ignore her comment and look at Devin. "Sure you don't wanna do 'Bohemian Rhapsody?' Pairs well with the weird little *I-just-killed-someone* vibes you're puttin' out there."

"Nah, everyone does Queen," Dolly says, decidin' for us, once again stunnin' me with the knowledge she's got crammed in that tiny little *American Girl* doll shell of hers. "Plus, the Stones' song is about Lucifer being behind the murders. You should go with Nick Cave if they got it."

"No one asked her. Let's do Phil Collins," I say, overridin' what the kid wants. I force a smile at Devin. "I'll be your echo and jump in on the chorus. I can probably pull off some stellar air-guitar on that one, too."

"Would you still wanna sit by me if I had?" Devin burps into his mouth and looks at me, eyes lookin' a little lost and mournful.

"What?" I'm confused. "If you had *what*?"

"...Killed someone?"

"Uhhhh." I don't know how to answer that. It was the last thing I expected him to say, frankly.

Devin has changed gears, like he'd forgotten he'd even asked. "Let'ssss go." He rises from his seat and twirls his finger around in the air. I decide to ignore his bizarre question, chockin' the nonsense up to inebriation.

We make our way down the carpeted steps toward Lawrence's booth. We line up behind a stout blonde woman with one of them lopsided half-haircuts who requests Swift's 'Shake It Off.'

Dolly and I glance at each other as she does. It's the kind of song I'd expect from Dolly-house, not a grown adult. Finally, the lady leaves, and we are up next in the queue.

"Putting in a song request?" Lawrence asks me, his eyes driftin' to the garage-door-sized openin' in the room leadin' to the hallway outside. His gaze seems frozen on the curvy, black-haired photographer who takes everyone's picture on the way in against a faux backdrop she's got set up just outside.

I snap my fingers in his face and raise my voice a little. "Hey, we're over *here*, bud."

This annoys him more than I expected. His lips purse and his jaw flexes. "Can you keep your voice down?"

"Excuse me?" I'm stunned. I didn't even think I was talking that loud. I turn to Dolly, who is followin' me around like a gosling. She raises a hand to her face to hide her satisfied smile.

"We get one set of ears, ma'am. When those are ruined, you're on a hearing aid forever. You don't need to be so loud."

"You're jokin', right? You work the sound booth at a karaoke joint!" I scoff, hopin' Devin will back me up with a laugh.

"I am aware that I do. I use high-quality hear-through earplugs when the *music is on*," Lawrence grunts, "*ma'am*."

"Okay, that wasn't the *polite* ma'am. That was the *rude* ma'am. Like the *Karen* ma'am." I start to fume.

Lawrence just stares at me. Finally, I take a deep breath and exhale. "'We're Not Gonna Take It.'"

"Take what?" he asks.

"No, that's my song. Twisted Sister. Write it down."

He laughs. I notice he doesn't write anything down. I just stare at him for a moment.

"Oh, you're serious?"

"...As my second heart attack, kid. I don't joke about karaoke or food."

He types somethin' on his laptop while he laughs and shakes his head. "Name?"

"Uma Blanchard."

He clacks some more keys. Then, he looks at Devin and Dolly. I speak for Devin. "We're doin' 'In the Air Tonight' by Genesis," I say, flashing my most supremely defiant glance at Dolly.

"You mean by Phil Collins?" he corrects.

I swear, I could reach across this booth and bop this kid's head with my closed fist like a whack-a-mole game.

But I don't…

"Yeah. Sure." I feel Dolly's eyes laser-burnin' two holes into the back of me. I don't dare turn around and look at her.

"Name?" Just as he asks Devin the question, his cell phone, a large one with an Anime case, starts to chime the familiar melody of an old Tommy Tutone song…

"867-5309/Jenny."

It flashes the words TAKE MULTIVITAMIN across the purple screen. He looks at it, confirms the time on his watch, and lays it back on the table with the giant Anime boobs facin' up at me.

Yecch… Men can not possibly think breasts *that* large are attractive. Not only are those doggone anatomically improbable, but that poor girl'd have horrendous back pain from carryin' around those watermelons all the time if she were real.

He fishes around in his pocket for a loose pill and pops it into his mouth.

"Best turn that ringer for those alarms off so you don't distract from the performances. I don't think the singers'd take kindly to that kinda interruption," I say curtly. And by singers, I mean *me*.

He nods absentmindedly, not makin' eye contact. He isn't listening. He's just humorin' me. After he washes the pill down with a swig of bottled water, he goes back to clackin' on his laptop keys.

"Um… Are we botherin' you?" I ask.

Lawrence shakes his head. "I asked for your *name*, didn't I?"

This rude little…

Devin speaks up. "Devin Cohelo. Oh, and Uma here."

"And your great-great-grandkid?" Lawrence asks, lookin' up at me. "She singing anything?"

"First off, I'm not old enough to have great-*great*-grandkids. Second, she isn't with me."

"She sure *looks* like she's with you."

"You ever go to the bathroom and get a length 'a toilet paper stuck to the bottom of your shoe?" I point over my shoulder at her.

"'Don't Bring Me Down' by ELO, please, sir," Dolly says sweetly, as if she's somehow had manners all this time.

Lawrence chuckles and then eyes the photographer outside the door again for a moment. "Yeah, fine. Go sit down. I'll call you when it's time."

***

Eighty-seven minutes of torture go by, in which time I check my mother-of-pearl watch about two hundred times, watch Devin order whiskey two more times, argue semantics with an eleven-year-old nine times, and hear three *separate* renditions of 'What's Up' by 4 Non Blondes, each soundin' more like a screechin' alley cat than the last.

Finally, just when the stocky chick in the flannel (who *better* have sued someone over that haircut) sings the last few words of her teeny-bopper song, I start to worm my way out of the booth with a series of grunts, jabbing Dolly out of the booth with a bony elbow.

"Break a hip, Uma!" Dolly says loudly.

"The saying is break a *leg*, kid," I huff.

"Oh, I *know*," she says, a glimmer of cruelty in her eyes.

"Next up is Dolly Haus," Lawrence announces in his most lackluster announcer's voice.

42

Dolly gleefully brushes past me and breaks into a full-blown skip.

"If this guy forgot to put our names on the list, I'mma kill him," Devin growls. He lets out a half-hiccup-half-burp while glarin' at Lawrence as he snaps a selfie with several tiers of drunken cruise-goers in the background.

"What the…?" I holler. "Hey, 'scuse me, Lawrence!" I waddle past the stage and slap my hands on the surface of his booth. "You skipped my song! An' then you skipped my duet with *him*!" I point to Devin.

"Hmmm. Strange. I don't have you on the list." Lawrence's eyes don't rise to meet mine. He acts like he's concentratin' on something on the screen of his phone that requires all of his focus.

"This one goes out to my great-great-great-great grandma, Uma. You'll see her at the hot dog eating competition on Sunday!" Dolly motions to me at Lawrence's booth and gives me an exaggerated wink.

The jaunty drum beat of 'Don't Bring Me Down' comes on and, in seconds, Dolly is singin' it, dancin' with the stage presence of someone who has had way too much time to binge all those talent shows on TV.

Audience members are cheerin' throughout the room. Blue and orange light beams are dancin' around the stage.

And wouldn't you know it…

The little psycho nails every word.

I turn back to Lawrence. "She signed up *after* us. *We* signed up after that broad with the ugly hair. You totally skipped both of us!"

"That can't be," Lawrence mutters to his screen. "I only skip people who are rude." His black eyes dart up at me and then off to the side to fixate on the photographer again. In the last hour-and-a-half, I've noticed him starin' at her about fifty times.

I look at her and lean in, growlin' at him over Dolly's falsetto chorus. "Look, Lawrence. You can either put us back on the list after the brat, or…"

"Or *what*?"

"Or… I can… go to your manager."

"Please do, *ma'am*. You should go talk to my manager. He would *love* to hear all about how you were rude and how nice I was for not ejecting you when you nearly burst my eardrums earlier."

"Burst your eardrums?! Son, you are in the wrong profession if my voice bothered your delicate sensibilities like that, you fragile little…"

He leans back and crosses his arms. "Go on. Please. Keep talking so I can lodge a formal complaint with my superior."

"How the heck are you in *hospitality* when you're this doggone rude?! You are aware you're on a cruise ship with payin' guests on it, right?"

"Do *you* sign my paycheck?"

"My cruise fee *pays* your paycheck."

"Sit down, ma'am." He waves me away.

"I could pay that girl out in the hall a visit, let her know you've been gawkin' her like a starvin' man might eye a prime rib."

Lawrence's expression turns mean, a silent threat.

Devin approaches, another whiskey in hand. As he steps toward the edge of the stage where the booth is, he trips over a clearly marked power cord for one of the amplifiers. He lurches violently forward, catchin' himself on a nearby amp stack.

"Good God, Devin. Careful, you klutz!" I grumble.

"What seemsss to be the problem?" he slurs, ignorin' me, starin' right as Lawrence. I wipe a dribble of spilled whiskey off the booth, marvelin' at how miraculous his recovery was. A fall like that would have shaken me, but he seems like it's just a normal everyday occurrence for him.

I take a deep breath and point to the host. "This dingus ain't lettin' neither of us sing! He says I was *rude* to him and too loud, so he skipped us."

Devin's face twists into an expression of fury, and he starts pointin' at Lawrence with the index finger of the hand wrapped around the drink, sloshing the liquid nearly over the top edge of the glass a few times.

"Are you kiddin' me? We waited our turn jussst like everyone else here. Sssssir, what gives you the right?"

Just then, Devin swings his hand in a wide arc and splashes whiskey on the keys of Lawrence's laptop.

In a flash, Lawrence is out of his cushioned chair, arms reared up like a sneaky wolf in an old cartoon. He has booze splashed all across his pressed, black uniform.

"Oh my God, get the man a napkin or somethin', Devin," I holler.

"Are you freaking *kidding* me?!" Lawrence growls, feral and angry. He lifts up his laptop and turns it upside down as Dolly finishes the song. Booze dribbles from the keyboard onto the booth's flat surface. He looks at Devin and hollers, "You moron!"

This enrages the intoxicated twenty-something. Devin slams his nearly-empty glass down on top of the amplifier stack and starts unbuttonin' his sleeves and rollin' them up with a furious look on his face. He gets a wild look in his eyes. "You wanna go right now? I ain't afraid to throw down."

"I'm not gonna fight you!" Lawrence seems shocked that this is happenin'. "I'm going to have you banned."

"Banned?" Devin laughs and spins halfway around like Lawrence has blown his mind. Suddenly, he turns back and starts to lunge. I grab Devin by the tail of his button-down shirt before he can get his weight into the motion.

"Devin!"

"Let me go! I'mma kill him!"

"That's enough!" I shove Devin. He stumbles two feet backward, trips over the power cable again, and falls this time, his legs smackin' the karaoke booth as he topples onto his back. The rest of the contents fly off the booth, and Lawrence's pens, phone, songbooks, spare mics, and headphones go flyin' onto the slightly uneven floor. The gentle sway of the boat pulls the pens beneath the amplifier stack inside a hungry one-inch gap. The water bottle rolls and slams into the bottom of the speaker's housing with a plastic crackle.

The music is over. Dolly is standin' center stage watchin' all of this, tryin' to muffle her giggles with her hand. The audience is frozen in mid-clap, watchin' this trashy scrap happen in real time.

"You, two… You're both *banned*! Get outta my lounge!" Lawrence hollers, glancing at the mess of booze and strewn items on the floor all around his booth.

"Now who's the loud one?" I huff.

"Now!" Lawrence screams at the top of his lungs.

"Smooth move, Ex-lax," Dolly says into the microphone while starin' at me.

"Security!" Lawrence screams, arms extended, pointin' to Devin with one index finger and me with the other.

5

I follow the hostess to my assigned table in the fancy Lido deck breakfast area, feelin' mild shame. I'm not sure how I'm gonna frame bein' ejected from the Hammerhead Lounge last night to Cosmo and my kinfolk.

The warm Gulf wind sweeps through my curls and wraps around my legs through the thigh gap in my salmon-colored sarong as my table comes into view.

Cosmo waves, his tan, strong hands carvin' through the hot summer air. His Hawaiian shirt is cracked open, and his muscular pectorals and gray chest hair are peekin' out of the opening. He's like what I imagine a Ken doll would look like if plastic could age with grace.

Daniel and Jane are scoldin' Duncan for a seemingly hash-brown-related offense, and Isa is wipin' what looks like ketchup and shredded potatoes outta her brown hair while starin' at Stokely.

At the end of the table, Alan and Marisol eat without sayin' a word.

Near them sits Devin. Dark hair, dark sunglasses, black T-shirt and shorts, sandals the color of worn pitch. His skin, however, is as white as a ghost. He sips beer from a green long-neck bottle. As he catches sight of me, he clumsily slides out from the table to pull out my chair. He motions for me to sit as if he's a driver hired to escort me into my limo.

"Thank you," I say. At least he has some manners, even if he is a hot mess.

He nods, making his way back into his seat. As he pulls himself back toward the table, he slams his knee against the post beneath so hard that it topples his beer and wobbles all our crystal glasses full of ice water. "Oh shoot!" He scrambles to pick up his bottle and drops one of his utensils on the floor, scatterin' his silverware loudly across his place setting, so he can sop up the mess with his fabric napkin.

"You're a disaster, kid," I mutter.

A waitress walks by, and I wag my hand at her. "Hun, I'm ready to order when you get a sec."

The woman U-turns and comes to our table with a smile. Her hair is tightly braided, and her white uniform is so crisp you could cut someone's finger to the bone with the pleats. "What can I get you?"

"Eggs Benedict and a mojito. Extra mint, extra lime. Top shelf rum, *Cher*."

"You got it."

"And another of these, please," Devin says, hoisting his empty green bottle in the air.

The woman nods and scurries off.

I smooth the starched fabric tablecloth in front of me and lay my napkin across my lap. I look at Devin as he finishes off what's left of his beer. "Havin' a little hair of the dog that bit ya?"

He nods.

I look at the drink in front of Cosmo and smile at the tall class of red liquid he's stirrin' with a stick of fresh celery. "How're the Bloody Marys here?"

"Not bad. This one's a tad bland. Little light on the vodka." Cosmo smiles, and it melts me a little.

"How's it compare to Daisy Dukes in the Quarter?"

"It doesn't. Nothing tops Dukes." He takes a sip of his drink and drapes one arm casually over the back of his chair.

"How'd y'all do at the casino last night?" I ask.

"We made out like bandits," Cosmo says. "I think collectively we're up about three hundred already."

"Red twenty-three, baby!" Isa grins. "My lucky number was hot last night."

"That's fantastic!"

I turn to my grand-spawn. "How was mini golf?"

Jane sighs and, in her too-quiet voice, mutters something about one of the kids throwin' a putter overboard and the other launchin' his ball at some random kid like a projectile. At least I *think* that's what she's saying. I never can hear half the words comin' outta her mouth. She talks at one notch above mute, but she always *looks* like she's talkin' normal. Drives me up the wall.

"How was karaoke?" Cosmo asks. "You get yourself a record contract yet?"

"No. Not quite. Soon enough, I'm sure," I joke. "It was… Interestin'. To say the least."

"What'd you sing?"

"Not a doggone thing." I look over at Devin, the leather back of my chair squeakin' as I turn. "How much of last night do you remember?"

"Honestly, not much. I was sauced. I remember sitting with you and some little rude girl and then putting in our request at the karaoke bar. Pretty much everything after that is a fuzzy haze."

"You remember threatenin' to kill the host or gettin' us banned when you lunged at the kid?"

"What?!" Isa asks, shocked. "You got *banned*?"

"Yep," I say, my eyes locked on Devin.

"No. I don't remember any of that." He shakes his head solemnly. "Doesn't surprise me, though. I'm so sorry if I embarrassed you."

"Eh. Have you met my *grandchildren*? I'm no stranger to bein' embarrassed publicly."

As if on cue, I see a hunk of cantaloupe fly past my face. I trace its origin to Stokely, who has a fist on the base of his fork which is laid over a sideways salt shaker, bein' used like some kind of colonial trebuchet.

The hunk of melon landed atop Marisol's sunny-side up eggs. She looks absolutely horrified.

"*Excuse* me," Alan says, perturbed, his voice low. But the kids are unfazed by it.

"Stokely, you missed!" Duncan says. Then, they both giggle.

"Case in point." I point to the kids. I look over at Daniel, who is on his phone. "Dan, you need to put those two on a doggone leash!"

Daniel puts his phone down and quietly reprimands his sons in the most half-hearted way I can imagine.

I dig my shoulder into the back of my chair to face Devin. "You know we gotta make this right with Lawrence. We gotta apologize or somethin'. There's no way I'm goin' this whole cruise without singin' my karaoke."

Devin nods. "I'll swing by and apologize this morning, if I can track him down."

"Good. You do that." As I turn back to face the others, I realize this means I should probably swing by the lounge at some point and eat crow with that little Anime-lovin' idiot, too.

Isa speaks up, askin' everyone at the table as a whole. "What do y'all have planned today?"

Cosmo tries to hide his handsome smile so he can appear as humble as possible. "Well, I met a nice fella at the casino last night. He's the producer for a few big-budget TV shows, if you can believe it. Small world. He's part of some pickleball league up there in New York City. He invited me to play today at the court up there on the sports deck."

"I'm going to the art auction if anyone's interested in joining me," Isa volunteers, lookin' at me and then Marisol.

Marisol responds quietly, "I think I'll just lie out on the sun deck over there with my book, but thank you."

"Same, but without the book," I say as the waitress lowers a beautifully-plated Benedict breakfast in front of me. The positive reviews were spot-on for this meal, too. "Thank ya, doll."

The waitress nods and leaves.

Then, I add, "I'm gon' get nice and tan on this trip if it's the last thing I do. I ain't goin' back to my room until I look like an overcooked beignet."

"Wear sunscreen, Ma," Daniel insists.

"Hey, why don't you focus on parentin' your own kids instead'a tellin' *me* what to do?" I snip.

Daniel puts his hands up in surrender. "Sorry for caring."

I sigh and nod at the kids. "What're you little monsters up to today?"

"Arcade," they say in near-perfect unison.

"And you're gonna *behave* while you're there, right?" Daniel asks them, his tone a weak warning.

"You're not goin' with them?" I ask, surprised they'd allow those little golems to run amok unsupervised after *years* of provin' over and over that they can't be trusted.

"No," Daniel rubs Jane's hand lovingly. "I scheduled the wife and me a couple's spa day as a surprise. She deserves to be pampered."

"Aww," Jane says quietly.

"Massages, facials, mud baths, the whole nine." Daniel plants a kiss on the back of her hand.

"Ballsy move," I say, shakin' my head.

Isa pulls a tri-fold pamphlet out of her beach bag on the floor. "I stopped by the concierge desk this morning to check out some of the port excursions and saw there's a seniors' singles mixer this weekend. Figured y'all might be interested in checkin' it out." She strategically places both pamphlets on the table equidistant between Cosmo and I like some kind of dare. Her eyes dart between her father and I. "Y'all should think about goin'."

Cosmo's eyes meet mine, and a soft smile graces his lips. He flips through the top one and then stuffs it casually in the pocket of his half-unbuttoned shirt.

Then, he looks at me and shrugs. "Eh, you never know. Could be fun."

6

I stare at Cosmo on the pickleball court through my tiny binoculars from my sneaky li'l spot on the ninth green of the Polished Pearl Putt Putt course. When I bought these things, I made myself memorize five different bird species so that if anyone caught me usin' 'em, I could say things like:

"Hold very still. I'm checkin' out the plumage on that Fluffy-Backed Tit-Babbler!"

Or "Dang, that's a huge Dickcissel!"

Or "Get a load of mean little Sandy Gallito over there, raisin' heck!"

Or "Holy cow! I never thought I'd see such a massive pair of Blue-Footed Boobies!"

Today, I'm pretendin' to look at a Tinklin' Cisticola (which sounds more like the lyrics in the bridge of a Savage Garden song than a type'a *bird*, but whatever).

In *reality*, I'm watchin' a bead of sweat dribble down the muscular curves of Cosmo's back. It slides down the faint scar grooves from his various stunt falls and paid car crashes and has almost reached his stark white shorts, ones that hug thighs so strong they could constrict a grown human to death like a boa.

I hear music growin' louder, like there's some sorta party bein' thrown on one of the lower decks. I hear people clappin' and cheerin'. Buster Poindexter's classic cruise jam carries up to me on the breath-stealin' air. I smile to myself as I look back through the lenses at my movie star neighbor.

"You sure *are* 'Hot, Hot, Hot'," I mumble quietly to myself as I chew my lip.

"Spying on a boy, Uma?"

The child's voice behind me scares me so bad that I scream-shriek the words, "Tinklin' Cisiticola!" I woulda dropped my doggone binoculars on the AstroTurf had it not been for the rainbow-beaded neck strap I made for 'em during some dumb *Beads & Bordeaux* boozy craft night my sisters forced me to take with 'em in Metairie a few weeks ago.

"Is that *old* person code for you whizzing in your diaper?" Dolly's laugh is shrill and headache-inducin'.

My shocked expression morphs into one of anger as I straighten my posture and tuck my beaded binoculars into my beach bag, as if stuffing it beneath the rolled-up taco-print towel can somehow mask the shame of gettin' caught amid my spy session. "Kid, you are like the stubborn *booger* I can't seem to flick off my finger. You can't do that!"

"Do what?"

"Appear like some kinda apparition, hauntin' me outta nowhere like that." I smooth my sarong and tidy my wind-blown curls in an attempt to compose myself. "I yelled the name of a *bird*, if you must know."

"I know. I did a report on animals of the Savannah last year in school." She looks around, serious. "Only… Funny thing is… This doesn't *look* like a Savannah. It looks like a floating barge of capitalism and liquor. We're a long way from the Congo, granny."

"What *planet* are you from?" I scoff.

"You got busted. Face it," she says smugly. Then, she grins, proppin' herself up usin' her upside-down putter like a cane. Her other hand pops a dimpled hot pink ball up in the air, over and over. She's wearin' a blinding, holographic one-piece bathing suit and a pair of highlighter-pink shorts that match her ball. "So… Which one is he? Please don't tell me he's the chubby, hairy *Serpico*-looking one over there."

Dolly points to the producer, who is strugglin' to keep up with Cosmo on the court. He, oddly enough, *does* look a little like a squat version of Pacino. I'll bet his voice sounds like tires on loose gravel.

"Dear Lord, no. Also, you're *eleven*. You shouldn't be watchin' *Serpico*."

She ignores what I said completely. "Oh, you're checking out the *Lancelot* guy? Oh, my God, girl, you don't stand a chance."

"*Lancelot*?"

"Yeah, the guy from season three of *Lancelot* who gives the queen the rose to try to lure her away from her cousin. I don't think he had a speaking part. He was just part of Chalamet's army. The queen's brother beheaded him before he got any real screen time."

"Never saw it," I lie. I know *exactly* what she's talkin' about. No one on this *planet* can fill out a medieval chain-mail costume like Cosmo Goodman can. The kid's got a good eye. The fact that she could recognize him shirtless in the blindin' sun from this far away impresses me a little. For a tiny demon, she's got some skill.

Cosmo smacks the ball and spins, his arms up in celebration. Suddenly, he is facin' us, his calloused hand shielding his icy blue eyes as if tryin' to see us better.

I spin around, my heart racin'.

"Uma?" I hear him holler from afar.

I scurry away as if I don't hear him. I turn the corner and scuttle into the wide stairwell headed down. I don't want to explain why I was watchin' him from so far away. Through the increasin' volume of the steel drum music ringin' out at the nearby deck party, I hear the patter of tiny feet and see the refractin' light from Dolly's light-up sneakers on the glossy white walls.

"Where are we goin', Uma?" She is beside me now, pickin' up speed. She seems to have ditched her putter and ball somewhere along the way, and she's on me like white on rice. The stairwell spits me out onto the Panorama Deck near the Cobia Pool, complete with twisted water slides painted to look like eels. Over a hundred adults are laid out on lounge chairs in the blazin' sun. Children are splashin' in the pool.

"*We* aren't goin' anywhere," I say as I beeline for a cluster of available lounge chairs. "Scram, kid."

I try to wave her away. I unfurl my taco towel and drape it across the chaise. I see Marisol thirty feet away. She manages a small wave and then presses her face back into her towel, her oiled back the color of bacon workin' its way up to a sizzle in a pan.

"I am not going anywhere until you sign us up for the contest," she says defiantly, kickin' back on the chair next to me.

"What contest?"

"The hot dog eating contest! I won the bet last night at karaoke, remember?"

"Oh, God, don't remind me of karaoke, kid! What a travesty."

"I can't believe they threw you out." Dolly laughs. "I'd have died from embarrassment."

"It ain't my first time gettin' ejected. Trust me, it gets easier the more you do it. I'm just upset because I'm dyin' to sing."

"You tried apologizing?"

"That's not really in my nature, kid."

"My teacher says sorry goes a long way."

"Your teacher's a liar. She's obligated to say stuff like that if she wants to keep her job. They gotta walk a tightrope to stay employed these days. It's a shame. Back in my day, teachers could beat you with a wooden plank if you smarted off to them."

"Yeah, I see that really worked wonders on shaping you into a polite human being," the kid says sarcastically.

"Shut up."

"You just keep making my case for me over and over again." She sits in glorious silence for a moment with her yap shut. My eyes roll the moment it opens again. "You should oil his palms a little."

"What on earth…?"

"Isn't that the saying? When you bribe someone?"

"No, it's *grease* his palms there, Tony Soprano."

The overgrown doll has a point, though.

I never thought about smoothin' things over with a little wad of cash…

"Give him a little money and maybe he'll 'forget' the whole thing," she says, usin' air quotes like she's a character in *Goodfellas*.

"Not the worst idea in the world. Might be able to pretend last night never happened for a ten spot."

"Ten bucks? Good Lord, you're cheap. Ten's insulting," she says, like she has any idea about jobs and the value of a dollar. "If you really wanna sing, I think you gotta shell out some dough."

7

Day 2 - *1:10 pm*
Hammerhead Lounge
Coral Reef Deck 6

"I don't need an entourage, kid," I say as the elevator dings and the doors slide open to the Coral Reef level of the ship.

"Are you kidding? I wouldn't miss you botching a bribe for the world. Don't mind me. I'm just here for the show."

I stomp my way down the glossy, tiled corridor in the direction of the Hammerhead Lounge while countin' the rumpled roll of cash from the change purse in my beach bag.

I've got a five, eight ones, and a fistful of quarters. I didn't think to bring more cash than that. Everyone takes a blasted credit card nowadays! I wonder if Lawrence has a card swiper. *No, that's silly.* No one takes a bribe that way in the movies. Secretly, I wonder if I should hit the ATM, but then I decide that if I wrap the ones in the five, maybe Lawrence'll think it's more than thirteen bucks.

I start to pass a photographer who looks vaguely familiar. She is drinkin' a bottle of water while starin' out one of the huge windows at the vast, watery horizon. She is the photographer I saw Lawrence starin' at last night. I approach her.

"Hey," I say. Then, I realize I have no idea what her name is. She smiles at me and caps her drink.

"Would either of you like your photo taken?" she asks in an almost comical New York accent over Buffett's "Margaritaville" seepin' through the overhead loudspeaker. Her hand motions to the screen-printed backdrop off to one side of the wide corridor. She's chewin' the wad of gum in her mouth like she's punishin' it for some sort of wrongdoing.

"Come on, Granny. Let's take one for posterity," Dolly says. "So you'll always have something to remember me by."

I look at the photographer. "I don't know this kid. We aren't related. I sure as heck am not her grandmother."

The woman laughs and grinds her molars on her chewing gum again. "Are you sure? I thought I saw both a youse sittin' together at karaoke last night."

"Yeah, about that," I say, leanin' in close to her. I shove out my hand. "Uma Blanchard, by the way."

She lets the camera dangle on the strap around her neck so she can shake my hand. "Jenny." She points to her name tag, which reads: Jenny Applebaum.

"That karaoke host was eyein' you like a dog eyes a T-bone."

Her demeanor changes almost instantly from bubbly to disgusted. "That's Lawrence Fordham. Kid's such a pain in my neck. Always staring at me. I keep trying to get the higher-ups to let me work the stage shows or somethin' so I don't have to be around him. Kid gives me the willies."

I step back a little. "Yeah, I just wanted to let you know. He wasn't being very slick about it."

"You kidding me? That creep was flat-out gawking at her," Dolly adds without provocation. Then, she breaks into a tap dance near the backdrop, her little sneakers glitterin' like strobe lights as she entertains herself.

"No one asked you," I grumble.

"No one ever does." She sounds strangely chipper.

"I can't wait until he's gone." Jenny shakes her head and looks past me in the direction of the lounge. Then, she looks back at us and hoists her camera up in the air. "How about a picture? You don't have to buy it, but I haven't had much foot traffic today. Everyone's been hanging out up in the sunshine, it seems."

I sigh. "Yeah. That's fine. As long as you know I'm not buyin' it."

"Noted," Jenny says with a pretty smile, still chewin' her gum like a cow chews cud. She swoops her black bangs out of her eyes and steps into position.

"Wanna do the Charlie's Angels pose?" Dolly asks me. Then, she shoves her shoulder back toward me and turns her hands into a pistol shape.

"Yeah, sure. Let's do that," I say, while simultaneously shakin' my head 'no' at Jenny and swirlin' my finger in the air as if to say:

Hurry up. Snap your doggone photo.

Jenny clicks the shutter and smiles. "Thank you both. It'll be up at the *Take That!* kiosk on the Lido Deck in a couple of hours if you want to see it."

"Thanks," I say. Then, without another word, I start down the long hall again and huff as I hear the squeak of Dolly's ridiculous shoes behind me. "Seriously, kid, what do I have to do to get you to scram?"

"You know what I want." She sounds outta breath from joyfully skippin' in zig-zags behind me.

God, I'd kill to have that kind of boundless energy again.

"I ain't signin' us up for some idiotic dog-eatin' contest. I am *not* fillin' up on garbage with all this good food around."

"I can't sign up without you."

"I don't care."

"We had a deal!"

"Life is full of liars, deal-breakers, and fine print, kid. Get used to it."

"Fine." She skips in wide circles around me as I carry on toward the lounge, her blonde curls bouncin' with every impact. "Tell you what. You sign us up for the contest, take one bite, act like you're full, and make it seem like it's taking you a long time to chew it because of your dentures."

I groan. "I do not negotiate with terrorists." Ironically, I say this just as the sign for the Hammerhead Lounge comes into view. The irony is not lost on me. I'm about to negotiate with another one right now…

Here goes nothing.

Or thirteen bucks, I guess.

I walk into the dark lounge. The aquatic sheet-metal silhouettes all around make me feel like I'm in some defunct aquarium. Music plays softly, some sort of reggae song that sounds like a million others.

"Lawrence?" I holler.

The absence of a response makes me roll my eyes.

Of course, he isn't in here. I'm gonna have to waste the rest of my afternoon trackin' this fool down elsewhere on the boat.

I walk out onto the stage and step behind the mic stand, the one place in the world that always jus' feels *right*. I flip the switch and thump the black wire grid to see if it's on. It is. I speak into it.

"Lawrence Fordham? You hidin' in here somewhere?"

The second after I ask, I hear a light thump and a wet gurgle from the host's booth.

"Someone over there?" Dolly asks, tiptoeing a few feet behind me.

As I approach, I am stopped cold in my tracks by the sight before me.

It's Lawrence!

On the floor. With a broken pole stickin' straight outta his chest!

He looks like he might have been crawlin' toward the exit, one arm outstretched and reachin', the other layin' at a weird angle beside his torso.

"Kid, go fetch help!"

"Is he…"

"Now!" I scream.

"Okay! Jeez!" Dolly takes off runnin', her little shoes flashing through the dim lounge as she heads back in Jenny's direction.

I take a step toward Lawrence, my heart racin'. He isn't movin'.

In the full minute or so it takes for Dolly to race to Jenny and back, I haven't moved a muscle. I've just stared at Lawrence, shocked that my cruise has taken such a bizarre turn, wonderin' if maybe I'm cursed or somethin'.

"Help's coming," she says, barely outta breath. I feel her shoulder brush my wrist as she walks past. She grabs one of the pens off of Lawrence's host booth, approaches his body, and hunches down like a runner in a startin' position. Her LED soles light up the horrid expression of betrayal on Lawrence's face. She points to his outstretched hand with the pen, jabbin' him near his wide-open eye with the back of it.

He doesn't blink or move.

"Yup. Dead," Dolly says with the certainty of a seasoned homicide detective.

"Get away from him, kid! You're muckin' up the crime scene!"

She ignores me. "It definitely isn't suicide. Can't be from that angle of entry. And from the positioning of the vic, it looks like he was stabbed and tried to crawl away for help." Then, calmly, she taps her red-and-green wristwatch and says, "According to Ariel here, it's 1:12 pm."

"Thanks, Dollhouse. I *needed* a four-foot-nothin' human Timex to tell me that," I mutter sarcastically.

She looks back at me like I'm an idiot. "I just meant we should note that his time of death has to be prior to that. You see his coloring?" She points to him with the pen. "This D.B. is fresh. He's still pink. If he'd been dead a while, he'd be more gray."

"D.B.?"

"Sorry. Cop talk. It's short for dead body."

"And jus' how exactly do you know all *that*?"

"*First 48* is one of my favorite shows of all time," she replies matter-of-factly.

"Your folks don't even *know* how much they're messin' you up by lettin' you just run wild and feral like this."

"Yeah, yeah." She scoffs and waves me away and leans over the body.

"You're morbid, kid."

"I'm curious. There's a difference."

"Not right now, there isn't. Now get away from the body!"

Still, she studies the scene. I approach, careful not to step in any blood. Less because I'm worried about trackin' footprints and more because I don't wanna have to throw away these sandals. They're comfy, and I've worn 'em in *juuuust* right. They're not new, but they still have enough arch support that my plantar fasciitis don't seem to wanna act up.

I begin to squat down by the child, but my knees start to make the sound of a rotted log fallin' against the forest floor, and I decide to stay upright. Heck, if I do get down safely, it may take a while to get me back up again.

I stare at the rod protrudin' from the young man's torso. "What in the sweet name'a Bacchus is that *thing* stickin' outta him?"

"That?" Dolly looks at me like I'm dumb again. "It's a selfie stick."

"What the heck is a selfie stick?"

"It's like… an extension pole that you clip your cell phone to to take pictures of yourself from further away."

"*That's* what those stupid things are called? I've seen 'em, I just ain't known anyone ridiculous enough to *own* one."

"This one's nice. Carbon fiber, looks like." Dolly teeters forward over the body to look at the stick, and I suddenly realize how morbid this whole thing is, "Brand says… Chromatica."

"Where's his cell at if it ain't in the selfie stick?"

"I don't know."

"Keep an eye out for it, would ya? It's got a busty cartoon gal on it."

Dolly glances around and then back down at Lawrence. "Maybe he's lying on it."

"Yeah. Maybe."

"Or maybe that wasn't *his* selfie stick. Could have been the perp's." She looks at me and when I don't say anything, she says, "Sorry, perp is short for perpetrator—"

"I know what perp means, you little goblin!"

"Jeez, sorry. Bite my head off, why don't ya?"

I look around at the lounge, scannin' for clues. "This is jus' great. I ain't even been on board yet twenty-four hours, and I already got banned from karaoke *and* wrapped up in another murder."

"Another?" Dolly whips her head around and gives me a look like she just caught a whiff of one of the urine-soaked alleys off Canal Street.

"Yeah, there was a whole mess with my son-in-law last year. Well, *almost*-son-in-law, thank heavens."

"Maybe you're cursed."

I laugh. "Oddly enough, kid, I was just thinkin' the same doggone thing."

The silhouette of a broad-shouldered man in a uniform cuts through the sunlight pourin' in through the large lounge door. As he approaches, I get a better look at him. He's bald. The kinda bald that looks like it's by choice, not genetics. He's built like a linebacker, and as he brushes past me, I realize he's a solid two feet taller'n I am. He looks gravely serious as he orders Dolly away from Lawrence's body. She complies and walks backward.

"Officer Smalls, *bajar la puerta*."

His accent is thick and I recognize a little of the Spanish he's speakin'. Something about a door.

"Yes, sir!" The younger man who followed him in hops to it and races back toward the entrance, punchin' in a code on a keypad and then holdin' a button down. The door starts to lower.

The bald officer checks Lawrence's throat with two fingers, searchin' for a pulse. He looks back at the man who followed him in and shakes his head solemnly. The man nods, knowin' exactly what it means.

It means *it's official.*

Lawrence is dead.

Well... Fudgecicle!

Shoot. I wonder if they have a backup karaoke host in case of situations like these...

The bald man rises, white shoes as gleamin' white as the rest of his uniform and just as shiny as the skin on his head. It looks like he massaged it with baby oil. The glare off it is blindin'. He surveys the scene as one of the men closes the elephant door to the lounge. Then, he turns to Dolly and I and forcefully shakes my hand.

"Rinalto Nunca. First Officer in charge of safety," he says with the faintest hint of a smile as he looks at me. Even though it is almost imperceptible, it is still a little over the top for such a grim occasion.

"Uma Blanchard," I finally mutter, pullin' my hand back out of his giant, gorilla-sized mitt.

He looks down at the girl and smiles. She barely comes up to the pockets on his starched uniform slacks. "Is this your…?"

"You gon' finish that question?" I scrunch my brows.

"I'm Dorothy. You can call me Dolly." Dolly extends her hand, and they shake.

"*¿Eres su abuela?*"

"Excuse me?"

"Sorry. English, I is not always so good. I mean to say, is she your granddaughter?" Rinalto asks.

I cackle. "Oh, dear Lord, no."

Out of the corner of my eye, I see Dolly narrow her eyes at me.

He glances back at the corpse behind him, selfie stick juttin' outta the man's chest and back. Then, his gaze shifts to the other officer who is now surveyin' the scene, payin' close attention to the blood on the floor, presumably lookin' for footprint partials. I don't have the heart to tell him that the only ones he's likely to find are mine and the kid's.

Rinalto barks somethin' to the man about "Operation Rising Star" and orders the man to preserve the scene. He pulls his walkie from his belt and growls, "Code Mike to de Hammerhead Lounge. Repeat, Code Mike. Over."

Then, he re-clips the walkie and turns toward me again, a smile creepin' up onto his tanned face as he eyes me like a juicy steak.

In his thick accent, he says, "I'm afraid my team and I are going to need to ask you both some questions regarding all of this. Can you follow me, please?"

8

"It's just right down this hallway," Rinalto says. As he turns to the first open room, he salutes the woman inside. She salutes him back, her uniform so starched I swear I could hear it crackle as she moved. The patches on her shoulders have fewer gold stripey things on 'em than Rinalto's do. I imagine he's her superior.

"Sir." Her hand flies away from her face in a practiced motion.

"Did Officer Smalls radio you about Rising Star?" Rinalto asks her.

"Yes, sir."

"Dis *poquito chiquita* ees Dorothy Haus," he says, sayin' her first name with three very distinct syllables. Then, he slides her forward into the art-and-window-less room like she's a rook on one'a them oversized chess boards. "I need you to get a full report from her, okay?"

"Sir, yes, sir." She salutes him again, and then she smiles warmly at the kid. "Hi there, Dorothy! I'm just going to ask you a few questions and get you back on your way so you can enjoy your vacation, okay?"

"Yeah, fine. Whatever," Dolly says with a shrug, eyein' me as Rinalto shuts the door and leads me further down a solid gray hall.

I pass a room on my right, one full of computer monitors. Each screen has four security camera feeds displayed on it. I stop and stare at it for a minute as Rinalto continues down the hall.

As soon as he realizes I've stopped and am snoopin', Rinalto clears his throat assertively with phlegm that says, *Quit looking at that, you nosy dingus.*

"Sorry, I's just havin' a peek-see-poo at the set-up you got in there," I say as I scuttle down to the door he's holdin' open for me expectantly.

"Have a seat, Ms. Blanchard." Inside the room, Rinalto points to a simple chair in another colorless cube that looks like one'a them police interrogation suites from my murder docs.

"Or… Is it *Mrs.* Blanchard?"

"It's *Ms.* Blanchard." I take a seat. The cold metal chills the bare back of my legs. This is why I normally hate wearin' shorts. Then, when I go to leave, my skin's gonna cling to the doggone thing like a bumper sticker.

"Oh." His voice goes up a little, like an outta-towner delightin' in his first benieght. I don't expect the Cheshire grin he flashes me as he sits. He looks oddly flirtatious, even though I must have fifteen or twenty years on him. He pinches his bare ring finger. "That explains why no ring."

"Why? Does that *matter*?"

"No, not for the *investigation*."

Oh, Lord Almighty…

He really is hittin' on me. I musta fallen asleep with my feminine wiles cranked up to *max* again! It seems my milkshake is bringin' all them boys to my yard.

"Ms. Blanchard, walk me through your day. Tell me everything from the time you awoke until now. Okay?" He pulls a pen and a small notebook from the skinny pull-out drawer above his lap and starts to write.

"Well, I should probably start a little further back and tell you what happened last *night*."

I spend a few minutes tellin' him pretty much my every move since dessert -- save for the little bird-watchin' fiasco this mornin' when Dolly scared me half to death. I make sure to tell him about Lawrence's beef with Devin and the altercation I broke up between them, too.

At one point, Rinalto is scribblin' the information so fast'n furious that his hand cramps. Glancin' over at his paper, I don't know how he's ever gonna be able to decipher that chicken-scratch he calls handwritin'.

After I've told him everything I can think of, I start askin' my own questions. "So, Nunca, are you like the cruise version of a cop or somethin'?"

He snickers, puts his pen down, and leans back in his chair like we are on some kind of awkward dinner date waitin' for the wine to arrive. "Yes, sort of. I am the head officer in charge of safety. In rare cases of incidents with fatalities, I lead the investigation until we arrive at the next port."

"What happens at the port?"

"The FBI arrives, and they take over the investigation from there."

"Ohhh, real-life FBI?" I get excited at the thought of meetin' one in the wild like this.

"Yes, real-life FBI, *cariño*." He gives me a wicked little smirk.

"What happens to the body when someone dies on a cruise ship?"

"Oh, don't worry yourself with the morbid details, Ms. Uma."

"No, seriously. You don't, like, chuck it in the ocean or somethin', do you?"

"*Que?* No!" He laughs.

"You don't," I lean in, my voice quieter, "put it in the galley's walk-in fridge or somethin', do you?"

"Ms. Uma, the body goes to our morgue right here on the ship. That is, until we get to the port in Cozumel. In the meantime, I am in charge of this investigation. And, if this is the kind of thing you find *attractive*, I must tell you, Uma…"

He leans forward and rests his weight on his muscular forearms. Beneath the short sleeve of his uniform shirt, I see the bottom half of a pin-up girl in a sailor uniform, poorly-drawn legs wrapped tightly around an anchor. His years of bein' in the sun have tanned it almost beyond the point of recognition. I only know what it is because one of Harold's old friends on the force used to have somethin' similar.

"I have my very own handcuffs and a private holding cell right here on this boat."

"Ohhhh-kay," I mumble, unsure if he's offerin' somethin' that would make me blush or if he's threatenin' to lock me up.

Either way, I'm not into it.

…Probably.

"Anything else you'd like to ask me? I am an open book." He clasps his hands behind his shiny head. I get the feelin' he wants me to inquire about him personally or ask if he, too, is single. I sure as *heck* am not gon' take the bait.

"Yeah. What's *Code Mike* mean?"

"It means bring a stretcher."

"Interesting." I chew my lip a little. "Let me ask you the million-*dollar* question, Cap'n."

"I'm the First Officer, but…" He waves his hands at me and leans back again. "Go on."

"Who's gon' be runnin' karaoke in the meantime now that Lawrence bought the farm? Is it gonna be someone nicer'n him?"

"I'm afraid there won't be any karaoke tonight. Actually, probably not for the rest of the cruise, unfortunately. The Hammerhead Lounge and all of the scheduled activities in it are now officially on hold."

In a flash, I'm fired up. "What?! Why?!"

"*Mamacita*, because that lounge is an active crime scene. We can't risk destroying any evidence until someone is brought to justice. *¿Entiende usted?*" He grimaces at his accidental lingual mix-up. "I mean to say, do you understand?"

"This is a buncha seagull crap!" I cross my arms and huff. "I waited a full doggone year to go on this-here cruise because of *one* dead body, and now that I'm on it, I can't even do what I came here to do because of *another* dead body!"

He scribbles somethin' illegible. "*Another* body? Tell me about this *other* dead body, Ms. Blanchard."

"There's nothin' to tell!"

I'm really gettin' flustered now.

"Look, my daughter's fiancé turned up dead last year right 'fore my cruise and I had to stay in Lose-yanna while those bumblin' *fools* at the police station sorted everything out."

"I see. So dead bodies... They turn up around you a lot, you might say?"

"I wouldn't consider two a *lot*."

"What number *would* you consider a lot?"

I stare at him for a moment before finally speakin', a rare occurrence in which my mind is engaged before my yap is. "Now just hold the phone there, Nunca—"

"Please, you can call me by my first name. Rinalto."

"You don't think I had somethin' to *do with this*, do you?"

He just stares at me for a moment. Then, his eyes drift down to the scribbles before him. "You said yourself that you had an altercation with him last night. This was not like you just stumbled upon some stranger dead in one of the lounges."

"Are you kiddin' me? I was *miles away* when this whole mess happened!"

"Can you prove it? Can anyone vouch for your whereabouts midday today?"

"Aside from that kid in the other room? I'm sure of it."

"I see." He scribbles somethin' else. Clearly, I haven't assuaged any of his suspicions.

"Look, don't get me wrong, I'd have *loved* to have slapped the guy around a little last night for bein' such a jerk to my table-mate and I at karaoke, but stabbin' someone through the torso for it? Son, I ain't got the strength for *that*! I can barely skewer a *kabob* when I'm grillin'. Hell, if it ain't a marshmallow for s'mores or a cheese cube on a party platter, I typically don't go around stabbin' things at all!"

"Well, when we play the security footage back and examine the evidence, you should be cleared right away then." He picks at somethin' nonexistent on the plain white table between us. "Until then, *Mamacita*, you know… Jus' don't leave the country."

There is a moment of silence between us before he bursts into one of the loudest cackles I have ever heard in my doggone *life*. Thank *God* I don't have hearin' aids yet because this moron woulda blown 'em out!

"I kid, I kid. You're on a boat!" He laughs some more. In his thick accent, he asks, "Jus' where are you going to go?"

Pffft. At this rate?

Overboard.

***

As I'm ushered out of the tiny room, I say, "Well, hurry up on this investigation. Some of us want to use that lounge."

"*Si,*" he says with a slight nod, as if he's humorin' me.

We walk the final stretch of the hall toward the main lobby, edged in mall-like shops full of glittery wares. Just as the excursions desk comes into view, I see the door to the room housin' all of the security monitors to my left. Thinkin' fast, I turn to Rinalto and use my feminine wiles to my advantage.

"Oh, Rinalto, I know this is gon' sound silly, what with me bein' a strong, independent woman'n all, but I'm still a little bit shaken. Seein' someone's eyes void of life is somethin' I don't think I'll ever get used to. You think I could get a hug from a big ol' protective man like you?"

I barely finish the words before Rinalto scoops me into his huge, vice-like arms. I feel like I'm bein' constricted by one'a them anacondas I seen on a Florida Man documentary. He squeezes me tight, like he never wants to let me go. As he does, I peer around the edge of his pressed sleeve through the round window to see if there's a feed for the Hammerhead Lounge.

Aha!

I spot a screen showin' the karaoke stage and several security officers in white weavin' in and out from the side of the screen. The angle gives a great view of the stage, but not of the booth area where Lawrence was murdered.

Hmmm. Maybe there are other angles I'm not seein'. With a ship like this, I'm sure there are eyes everywhere. Someone would have to be an absolute *fool* to think they could get away with a murder on a cruise ship as big as this.

Rinalto pulls away just enough to smile down at me, and I'm forced to tear my gaze away from the security feeds.

"That was nice. I think I needed that, too," Rinalto says. Then, after a pause, he leans down toward me just and inch and I jerk away from him in a violent fashion.

"Thanks for the hug," I say, mostly just to get the big oaf away in case he was tryin' to kiss me.

He straightens and steps away, still smilin' wolfishly. "If I have any more questions, we will be in touch, Ms. Uma."

"You gon' send me a message in a bottle or somethin' to get ahold of me?" I joke, a glaring fail at some nautical humor. *Not my best work.*

"Oh, don't worry, Ms. Uma. *I will find you*," he says it more ominously than he intended, I'm sure. I think he was tryin' to be flirty again, but it came off a little stalker-ish. Either way, it's a weird end to a weirder interaction. "Enjoy your cruise, *Mamacita*."

I force a smile that probably comes off more like my Chihuahua's snarl when I'm tryin' to force him to take a pill he don't like the smell of.

"Uh, yeah. Toodles," I say with a wave, and his large form retreats back into one of the offices at the far end of the hall. I let out a big sigh of relief that now I can go back to enjoyin' my cruise in peace, albeit one livin' karaoke host shy of what I'd consider a good time.

On my way out to the lobby area, I walk past the room Dolly's bein' interrogated in. She looks at me through the little porthole thingy on the door, and I stick my tongue out at her.

Ha-ha. I got out first. Good luck findin' me now, clingy little sucka!

In the lobby, my eyes scan the ridiculously-overpriced wares in the shop windows, all glitterin' beneath the light of the chandelier hangin' over the excursions desk. My eyes drift to somethin' super-shiny in one of the windows: a baby-pink stone-encrusted snorkel and mask set. I'll be dipped. How much is this garish monstrosity? The price tag says…

Oh, *salt my roux.*

Four hundred and some-odd-dollars.

I am always amused by what rich people'll spend their hard-earn dimes on. It looks like somethin' Elton John might pack for a vacation to Maui, and I can't seem to look away.

I laugh, shake my head, and shuffle off.

9

Day 2 - *4:37 pm*
The Gills Swim-Up Bar
Lido Deck 9

"Hey, handsome. Gimme a mojito. Extra mint, extra lime. Top shelf rum." I narrow my eyes at the devilishly handsome young man behind the bar. "I'll be able to *tell* the difference."

"You got it," he says with a smile that only lands on half of his face. *My heavens, if I were about thirty years younger…*

"What's ya name, *Choupi*?"

He steps back from the swim-up bar in the shallow end of the Cobia Pool to a dry overhead cabinet and pulls a clean glass out. He sloshes through the water back over to me.

"Marvin Button, ma'am." He sets the glass on the bar in front of him and gets to work on the drink. "And you?"

"Uma Blanchard."

"Where are you from, Uma?"

"Just outside'a Nawlins. Little town called Killjoy. You?"

"L.A."

"That explains the movie-star good looks."

He blushes a little. Then, he stops muddlin' the mint and simple syrup for a moment to point at my swimwear. "It's not every day I see a *Mr. Potatohead* bathing suit."

My brown one-piece has printed-on eyes between my boobs, a red oval nose, and a cheesy smile partially covered by a black mustache, just like the classic toy. "I got a pear-shaped body and a sense of humor. Figured I could really nail the resemblance."

"I had one of those in my toybox when I was a little kid."

"Oh, so that was what? Last *week*?" I joke. He's not *that* young. Probably in his early thirties, but the boyish haircut and flawless skin make him look youthful.

He splashes in some lime juice, selects a bottle of rum off the top shelf of the bar, and eyes himself in the mirror behind it for a moment. Can't say I blame him. If I looked like that, I'd probably be obsessed with my own reflection, too.

He turns and flings the glass rum bottle into the air behind him. It flies up end-over-end a few times, arcs over one of his defined deltoids, and then returns effortlessly to his hand.

I offer a golf clap and my best De Niro impression, impressed. "Nice trick. I'mma call you 'Cocktail.' Movie's probably a *touch* before your time, though."

"Oh, I've seen it a lot of times. Had a *massive* crush on Elizabeth Shue growing up." He sloshes through the water back to my glass and starts pourin' in the rum.

I mumble, "Don't be afraid to go heavy with it. It's been a helluva day."

His brilliant smile morphs into a slightly more solemn expression. "Same here."

He gives the rum a heavy-handed pour and presses a finger to his lips like it's a secret that he gave me a little extra. He stirs in some ice and fills the rest with club soda before volunteering, "We just lost a crew member today."

I perk up at this, and then try to pretend it's news to me. "Oh no, who was it?"

"This guy I've known for a few months. He usually hosts karaoke in the lounge."

I pretend I don't know what he means by the word *lost.* "That's rude. He just up and quit on y'all?"

"No." Marvin garnishes the glass with a thick slice of lime and a sprig of mint, slaps the side of the glass once, and slides the drink to me. He leans across the half-submerged tiki bar, restin' on his bronze forearms.

"He..." Marvin looks around, rolls his eyes up in his lids, and sticks his tongue out like he's trying to get me to say 'dead' in a round of Charades. "I meant, like, lost him as in *permanently.*"

"Oh," I pretend I am catchin' on. "Like, as in *dead* lost?"

"Mmmm-hmmm. As in *met his maker*." Marvin doesn't seem too fazed by the permanence of his co-worker's leave. Maybe he's in shock.

"*Pauvre bête*. You don't seem too upset about it."

He laughs and then tries to compose himself instantly. "I'm not. I hated that guy."

I squint at him, tryin' to judge whether or not he could have killed the man.

"Oh yeah? Why's that?"

"Dude was so obnoxious. Acted like he knew literally everything about everything. He lives to correct people." He scrunches his face. "*Lived*. Wow. Can't hardly believe it's real."

"He sounds like a real gem."

"Ugh. All he did in his free time was try to make music for video games on his computer. Like any self-respecting game designer would ever use his stuff. He would get so upset, too, if people were loud around him."

I pretend I didn't learn this the hard way firsthand last night in the lounge. I nod, listenin'.

"It's like, dude, you work in a karaoke lounge! It's like the loudest part of the ship."

I wanna scream, *I know! What the heck?!*

Instead, I nod again.

"Anyway, whatever. I shouldn't speak ill of the dead." Marvin wipes droplets from the counter with a dry rag, and it almost makes me laugh out loud because we're both up to our waists in pool water.

"Dyin' doesn't give one a free pass to live like a jerk. People remember the dead too fondly, in my opinion. We turn them into martyrs and saints, even if we wanted to choke them out half the time." I suck down a large portion of my mojito in one drag through the black straw and moan as I point to the glass. "Bang-up job, Cocktail."

"It's good?" He grins.

"Best one I've had yet." I take another sip and slap the bar with my wet, chlorine-scented palm.

"I'm glad."

I look up from my drink to see that Marvin now has his phone in his hand. "Mind if I take a selfie of us with the drink for the socials?"

"Socials?"

"Social media." He bobbles his head, and his bangs bounce. "Oshannic has us post to the socials several times a day. Plus, they give out a bonus to whoever posts the most over each cruise. Right now, I think I'm tied for first with one of the ushers who works in the Coral Theater."

"You guys have a *quota* for how many pictures you have to post online in a day?"

He nods. "It gets cruisers excited. Keeps the platforms pushing our content every time people engage with the stuff." He grins. "I'm sorry. This is all hashtag boring."

"Nah. Tell you what." I suck down the bottom half of my mojito all at once and wince at the brain freeze. "Make me another just like that, and I'll cheese for however many of those stupid snapshots that you want."

"Yeah?" His bleached-pearl teeth shine in the settin' sun. He points to my booze card. "I can't give you another free one til your ninety minutes are up. They got cameras all over this place, unfortunately."

"Oh, I know." I say it so confidently that Marvin cocks his head like a Labrador. I wave him off, not wantin' to explain that I just saw the monitoring room a couple hours ago. "These days, there's cameras everywhere. Surprised they don't have one in the *can*." I scoff and toss him the lanyard around my neck that holds my alcohol pass and room key on the clip together. "Bill this one to my room. I gotta rinse the rest of this day outta my mind."

"Comin' right up." Marvin takes my empty glass in one hand, turns his back to me, and shoves his camera way out. He angles it up high and takes a selfie of us together, the ripplin' aquamarine water of the pool framin' us.

"You should get yourself one'a them selfie sticks," I say as he tucks his phone back into an overhead cubby beneath a stripe of tan, straw-like fringe edgin' the top of the tiki bar.

"Yeah," he chuckles to himself. "I had one around here. A pretty nice one. I don't know what happened to it. Darned thing's gone missing."

Despite the warm water lappin' at my spandex-clad buns, I feel a chill rush through me at the comment. I try to laugh it off, but it comes out soundin' like I'm under duress, forced to laugh with a gun to my head.

"Your shift over soon?" I inquire.

"No. We work long hours. The swim-up doesn't close until seven. Then, I move inside and tend at the dueling piano bar on the Gulf Deck."

"When did you start workin' at Gills?" I ask, tryin' to see if Marvin has a decent alibi.

He stuffs another big sprig of mint into the concoction he's whippin' up. "I think I got bumped up to the swim-up bar last June."

"No, I meant today. When does your shift at this bar start?"

"Tomorrow, I'll be here from one to seven, I think."

I snicker and then swirl my hand in the ripplin' water beside my submerged bar stool. "What hours did you work today?"

He cocks his head again and stares at me, as if what I said is curious. "Why?"

Uhhhhh… Fudgecicle! I have no idea what to say. Finally, I settle on a lie.

"Oh! Uh, 'cause I thought I saw you up at that little bar by the pickleball courts this mornin' serving bloody Marys. If your mojito is this proper, I'll bet you make a darned good one of *those*."

"I *do* make a mean bloody Mary. Spicy as all get-out. And I do *not* skimp on the garnishes."

"I'll bet you don't."

Marvin looks out at two screamin' boys just past the pool. Without even lookin', I can already tell by the sound of Stokely's shrill shriek that Duncan is tryin' to low-key murder him with a deck full of witnesses. I see a stocky crew member march in that direction, and I hold still so that no one can even loosely connect me to those two juvenile heathens.

"Friggin' unruly kids. Parents don't raise 'em right these days." I scoff, shieldin' my eyes with my hand as my grandchildren are marched away, one of their drippin' arms firmly in the grasp of a crew member. I wonder how long it'll be before they get ejected off the boat and dumped at a nearby port on a pathetic dinghy with Daniel and Jane.

"But no," Marvin continues after the long pause. "Wasn't me you saw. I worked the limbo party on the Panorama Deck this morning. I got here right after."

He slides the finished drink over to me, and I hoist it. "Thank ya kindly, Cocktail."

"You got it," he says with a charmin' wink, and suddenly, I've forgotten my whole line of questionin'.

10

Three strong mojitos down and I am feelin' groovy. I drag my hands along the textured wallpaper between what feels like three hundred staterooms pretendin' I'm capable of walkin' in a straight-ish line. I need to get changed into something more presentable for dinner.

I pass Cosmo's door and smile at the engraved plate with his room number. Number 1975.

Good year for music.

I eye the maid cart stationed in the hallway across from my room before I slide the key on my lanyard over the sensor. It beeps, and the green light flashes. I open the door.

A red-headed man with a scraggly rat-tail braid whips around. His fair, freckled skin is sunburned to hell, and he is standin' at the foot of my bed foldin' some kinda terry cloth animal.

I scream. It is the first and only instinct that seems to make sense right now, after all that rum. The sudden sight of the stranger in my room makes my feet come all the way off the floor like a spooked cat for just a split second.

"*Mais là!*" I exclaim, clutching my poundin' chest.

"I'm sorry!"

"What're you doin' in my room, *Cher*?!"

The man puts his pale, doughy palms up in the air like I'm aimin' a gun at him. "I'm hospitality, ma'am!"

"Oh my God." I double over and laugh. "A maid? Chile, you scared me half to death."

"I'm sorry. I was just doing turn-down service." The man starts to rush out of the room like he's just been caught doin' something illegal. Good thing I don't have nothin' decent in there for him to steal. Even my jewelry ain't worth more'n a couple bucks. It's all rhinestone and faux gold. The stuff'll turn your skin shamrock green if you wear it after a shower.

"What's your name, son?" I feel like I'm startin' to slur. I need to get some good food in me stat.

"Drew."

"Drew is a past-tense verb, not a name, son."

He just stares at me.

"You got a last name?"

"Pye, ma'am."

I shake my finger like I'm about to teach him a lesson. "Well, Drew Pye, you need much longer in here? I'm tryin' to get changed for dinner."

"I just finished. All yours."

"Thank you for your service," I say with reverence. "I used to be a hotel maid, a million lifetimes ago. I know it ain't easy."

Drew doesn't respond. He just darts nervously past me, nearly shoulder checkin' me as he rushes out. He grabs his cart and shoves off down the hall in a hurry.

Ohhhhhhh-kay.

Odd boy, that one.

11

On my way to *The Knotty Buoy* restaurant for dinner, I happen to pass by the *Take That!* photography kiosk. Near the wide opening of the store, I see a factory-sealed selfie stick hangin' on the wall. Gray. Carbon fiber. Extendable. It looks exactly like the one I saw stickin' outta Lawrence this mornin'!

Just as I go to take it off the metal wire, I hear, "Good to see you again, ma'am!"

I recognize the New York accent almost immediately. I whip my head so fast my neck cracks.

It felt good, actually.

Maybe I should try doin' that more often.

Jenny Applebaum waves frantically from behind the register. I approach and glance up at the walls of photographs of cruise-goers posed in front of various printed backdrops.

"Yeah, you as well. How ya holdin' up? You know, after the…?"

Jenny looks at me, confused, then realizes what I'm talkin' about. "Oh! It's still a little surreal, you know? I just saw him this morning."

"What for?"

"We were in the boss's office for a disciplinary meeting."

"Disciplinary meetin'? For you?"

"No," she laughs, "Lawrence. It was him, me, Cooper, and some of the higher-ups. We all had to sign paperwork and witness Lawrence gettin' his final disciplinary write-up," she says. "They called a big meeting. It was so awkward."

"What was the write-up for?" I ask, nosy as always.

I can't help it! I am who I am.

"He'd been borderline stalking me on the boat the last three cruises. He'd gotten in trouble before for being kinda creepy with some of the girls, but about a month ago, he got a little laser-focused on me in particular. Guy was always leering. He was infatuated."

"Yeah, his doggone eyes were glued to you last night durin' karaoke. I thought he was gon' get a crick in his spine from rubberneckin' that long."

"He was kind of a creep. Used to harass me. Leave little letters for me under my stateroom door. He'd request shifts on different decks so that he could be close to me. He annoys everyone. That's why he ended up getting exiled to the Hammerhead Lounge. He was relentless. A dog with a bone. It was even starting to cause problems with my boyfriend."

"Does your boy toy work on the ship?"

Jenny nods.

"Is he a photographer, too?"

"No. Hospitality." She watches a woman in a sarong breeze in, look at a photo of herself, and then waltz back out without ever makin' eye contact.

Jenny returns her attention to me. "He knows I'd never cheat on him, but still, it was creating tension."

"Think your boyfriend coulda done the deed?"

Jenny looks at me like I slapped her in the face. "Absolutely *not*. He's not confrontational enough to argue over the best flavor of ice cream, much less *kill* someone."

"What's there to argue? It's Rocky Road. Anyone who doesn't agree is jus' wrong."

Jenny ignores my comment, clearly not a fan of Rocky Road. "He wouldn't hurt a fly. Neither would I. I wanted Lawrence to buzz off, not *die*."

I'm not sure I really believe her. She was, after all, standin' right around the corner from where Dolly and I discovered his impaled corpse. Surely, she would have at least heard him scream.

Plus, if Lawrence was infatuated, that gives her or her boyfriend a reason to want Lawrence gone for good.

"Did Lawrence have any *friends* on this boat?"

Jenny shrugs. "To my knowledge, just Cooper. And even that was wearing thin."

"Cooper? As in Nagilnick? He the red-headed hobbit-lookin' guy?"

Jenny nods and chuckles softly. "Wow. Weirdly accurate. Now I'll never be able to look at him without thinking of *Lord of the Rings*. Yeah, he's the Funtivities Director."

"Why was his friendship wearing thin?"

"Man, you ask a lotta questions." Jenny leans in a little. "They used to be best friends, I guess. Cooper stuck his neck out and got him hired on with Oshannic a while back, but Lawrence has been a pain in everyone's butt the whole time he's worked here. Over the last few months, Cooper's been losing his patience, always having to bounce the creepy little loser from department to department until Lawrence inevitably screwed things up *there*, too."

I point to the photos with the package for the selfie stick. "Lemme ask you a question."

"Another one?" She laughs.

"Are these-here cruise photos timestamped somewhere?"

"They are. On the back."

"Where's mine and the kid's from earlier today? The one you took of us."

Jenny comes out from behind the register and hunts through some prints on a thin shelf just above my head. "I think yours is… *aha*. Right here."

She hands it to me, and I laugh. Dolly is makin' her fingers into a pistol with her back to me, Charlie's Angels-style. I'm not playin' along, arms folded across my chest in protest.

Ha... Fitting.

I flip it over and look at the back. It's stamped with the date and time, as well as the name Jenny Applebaum, the photographer.

"How much is it?"

"Twenty-five. Plus tax."

"Lord almighty," I mumble as I stare at it. That's too much money for a picture of a kid who annoys me, but it's also proof of my whereabouts and blood-free attire at a time when Lawrence was lyin' dead on the same ship deck. The way Rinalto looked at me today when I mentioned the karaoke kid bein' the second corpse I found in a year makes me wonder if I should collect all the evidence I can to back up my alibi.

But still...

Twenty-five dollars!

Ugh, too rich for my blood.

"I may have to send that First Officer fella, Rinalto, up here to see it at some point," I say as I stuff it behind some other eight-by-tens on the shelf in front of me. "You know they found his body near where you took that, right?"

"Yeah, they were questioning me about it earlier, actually. They thought I might have been the one to kill him."

"Were you able to prove you didn't?"

She nods.

"What was the proof?"

She stares at me for a second. "The timestamps." She points to the wall of photos in front of me, each with the same background as the one of Junior Fingerguns and me. "I didn't have many people wanting their pictures taken, but I had enough that they could tell I was there the whole time."

I nod. She didn't seem shaken when she took my picture. She'd have to be some strange level of psychopath to murder someone and act *that* relaxed mere minutes later.

I hold up the selfie stick package. "You sell a lotta these?"

"No. Most people come on the cruise having already bought one. Other people just, you know, use their arms."

I snicker at that. "You sell any recently?"

"Sure. We sell three or four each time we set sail."

"You remember who you sold 'em to?"

Jenny laughs. "No, ma'am."

"Hey, baby, I brought you a little something. They didn't have the Taro Milk Tea you like so I got you the Thai with the little brown sugar bobas you like," a man says.

My eyes widen when I see him.

"Hey, I know you," I say, starin' at the brown eyes squinting atop his two ruddy, puffy cheeks. "I never forget a rat tail."

Drew Pye stares at me like a scared opossum frozen in my Buick's headlights.

"You're my maid," I announce.

"*Housekeeper*," Drew corrects, lookin' embarrassed. He forces a slight nod and backs away from Jenny a little.

Skittish little fella.

"Aww," Jenny says, takin' the milky drink from his hand. She raises the straw toward her mouth and then stops. "Wait, is this Thai or Chai?"

"*Thai.*" The annoyed way Drew says it, I can tell there's some tension between them, some distance they're tryin' to span. It feels like they're makin' up after a fight. "I know you don't like the Chai. You made that clear last time."

"Okay, I was just asking. Jeez." She takes a big swig from the oversized straw. I watch as black circles rush up like aerator bubbles in a fish tank.

"Eww, is that that drink with them squishy balls in it?" I ask.

Jenny nods, still slurpin', acting like she's died and gone to heaven.

"How the heck can you *drink* that stuff? It's like vacuumin' up sugar loogies with a tiny hose."

"Sugar loogies?" Jenny laughs.

Drew doesn't. He just stares at me like I have offended him. I can't help but notice that he's barely makin' eye contact with his *own* girlfriend either, though. Maybe he's just a weird guy who doesn't know how to be friendly with anyone. Or maybe there's somethin' going on with these two…

"Oh my God, it's delicious. You should try it sometime. *The Boba Factory* on the Gulf Deck makes the *best* milk tea on the planet."

"It's her favorite," Drew mutters, lookin' like he'd rather throw himself overboard than be here right now.

"It's so good. You really are missing out."

"The only slimy thing that belongs in this yap is a fresh-shucked oyster, *Cher*." I sigh. "Great! Now you got me thinkin' about oysters! I should go on and git before my stomach starts a-growlin'. I got a dinner rezzie at *The Knotty Buoy*. I hear their fish and chips are outta this world."

I hang the selfie stick package back on the wall. Jenny tucks her drink on a shelf behind the kiosk.

"I gotta go, too," Drew mumbles, headin' back out the side opening of the kiosk. "I'm scheduled to usher at the Poseidon, and I still gotta get changed into my black uniform."

"Okay. Thanks for the drink, babe," Jenny says.

Drew mumbles somethin' unintelligible and jogs off in the direction of the stairwell.

"Interestin' choice." I look at Jenny and point in the direction he ran off. "Frankly, *Cher*, I think you're sellin' yourself short. You could do way better."

12

Day 2 - *8:00 pm*
Minnow Pool
Lido Deck 9

Stuffed from the whole basket of beer-battered cod and fresh fries in my belly, I waddle past the overly-nautical kitsch-filled walls covered in crab traps and distressed life preservers out the front door of *The Knotty Buoy*. I have no regrets about the amount of food I just ingested, an amount some might consider shameful. Thank the voodoo Goddesses above for this miraculous metabolism of mine. Otherwise, I'd be in a heap'a trouble, weight-wise.

I shuffle out into the hot summer air and make my way to the chrome railing, starin' out at the vastness of the ocean. I feel like a tiny pearl in this unfathomable amount of liquid.

Children splash in the Minnow Pool nearby. As I spin around and lean against the rail, I see familiar faces. Jane is lyin' out on a chaise lounge in a hat so doggone big it could shade three heads. Her face is half-buried in some bland-lookin' romance novel. Daniel's in the chair next to her, completely engrossed by somethin' on his cell phone.

Meanwhile, in the kiddie pool, Duncan is smackin' some strange girl in the face with what I suspect is her own inflatable pool toy. No one seems to be responding to her screechin' pleas for help to get it back, either.

Stokely is in the deeper end, starin' hard at some nappin' old man's wadded-up trousers near the leg of his chair. He is no doubt wonderin' if he could slide out, beach himself like a seal, and rob the wallet inside of all the cash without alertin' anyone.

"May I have your attention, please?" Cooper Nagilnick's overly-enthusiastic voice booms through a nearby amplifier. Everyone turns to him as he climbs up on top of a tiny wooden stage. "Aspire cruisers, it is time for the Oshannic Fiesta Dance Party! Here we go! Up on your feet, everyone! The train has arrived!"

Suddenly, a train horn toots and the old man Stokely was watchin' awakens from his slumbers, wipin' a trail of drool from his wrinkly face. Stokely slips back into the water until just his narrowed eyes are above the surface. *Rats, foiled again*, is what he looks like he's thinkin'.

Once the train whistle stops, the Ojays' song "Love Train" starts blastin' through the amplifiers and suddenly everyone is springin' to life to join in the conga line. I watch from the sidelines as a throng of strangers congeals, formin' a line that snakes through the chairs, pool area, and food court tables.

Cooper is the conductor scoopin' everyone up on his path through the deck. He passes and waves for me to join in. Just as I start to shake my head, I'm yanked into the line by a pair of strong hands. Cosmo smiles down and jams me into the line in front of him. He leans down, speakin' lowly into my ear.

"I haven't seen you since breakfast, Uma Mae. Where've you been?"

"Oh…"

I don't know how to answer that.

Um, *you know, findin' dead bodies in the karaoke lounge…*

Dodgin' the flirtatious advances of the First Officer in charge of safety…

Tryin' to establish an airtight alibi for myself…

"I've been around," I finally say. "You just ain't looked for me very hard."

Our conga line passes Devin Cohelo, who dips into the line in front of me, sloshin' the booze in his hand over the lip of the coconut it's poorly contained in. It smells like sunscreen and cheap rum. He wobbles joyously, clearly sloshed.

"What did you do today?" I yell back at Cosmo.

"Played some pickleball and went to lunch with that producer I was tellin' you about. Then, Isa and I caught the matinee of that circus show in the Poseidon Theater. I spent the rest of the afternoon in the pool with the kids. That Duncan…" Cosmo holds out a tan arm with an arc of small, red lines on the meat between his thumb and index finger, "he's quite the biter."

"He's worse than Cocodrie," I holler. "But at least Cocodrie's had his *rabies* shot!"

Cosmo laughs, and the sound warms me. That is, until Devin smashes my insole with his heel dancin' like a fool!

"Oh my God, I'm sssorry, Uma," he slurs as I hop around in pain. I fall outta line and grab onto a cafeteria chair. Cosmo comes to my rescue.

"You okay, Uma Mae?" Cosmo's hands slip around my upper arms to stabilize me.

"I'm fine. This dum-dum's just *sauced*, that's all." I point to Devin.

Devin looks at me apologetically. "I'm so sorry, Uma. I'm such a klutz." Then, he starts punchin' himself in the forehead *way* too hard. The hollow, bony sound of the *thump* is alarmin'. Kid's gonna end up with a big ol' welt whackin' himself in the noggin like that!

The Ojays' song fades into one by Kool and the Gang, and the flesh parade disperses, creatin' a chaotic mess of dancers all around the pool and buffet. It makes me think of buckshot fired into gelatin, the way they scatter.

I dance with the crowd, hopin' to work off some of my fried fish. It isn't until I see Cooper slink back toward the railing that I decide to break away. Jenny made some interestin' points today at the photography kiosk, and I feel the need to ask Cooper some serious questions. Although, the jovial atmosphere of this full-blown party hardly seems like the time to get a straight answer outta him. The guy is the Funtivities Director, after all. He's always movin' around on the ship like a doggone hummingbird, hosting stuff. I don't know if the next time I track him down is gonna be any easier to get him to shoot straight with me.

I need a diversion. Somethin' to get him out of this alleged *fun* zone and somewhere quieter.

I look around at the dancin' people, the ripplin' pool, the lonesome buffet of coolin' food…

Then, I see *Dolly*.

Sittin' on a lounge chair by a comatose middle-aged woman who looks like she overdosed on Valium.

I dance around the pool toward the kid. She sees me, and I beckon her the rest of the way with a finger. She suddenly sparks to life, her once-sad face vibrant and mischievous now. She skips over to me and I pretend to dance with her, starin' down at her light-up sneakers.

"That your momma?" I ask, noddin' in the direction of the passed-out female.

"That *was* my mom. About a bottle-and-a-half of *prosecco* ago." She frowns and then looks back at me. "She'll be dead to the world a while."

"I could use your help, *Cher*."

Dolly scrunches her face like I just called her some kind of slur.

"Excuse me? You reneged on the hot dog eating contest already and left me with those creeps during the interrogation earlier. Why on *earth* would I wanna help you?"

Despite her words makin' it sound like she hates me, her body is dancin' like she's auditioning for a musical. She's like that Bacon guy in *Footloose,* and her light-up shoes are squeakin' on the damp planks like the springs of an old bed. Her feet are movin' so fast, I'm waiting for her soles to start smokin'.

"Sign us up for the contest, and I'll forgive all the other crud," she orders. Then, she points to a woman on the other side of the small stage. "The sign-up booth is right over there."

"How convenient." I sigh. "Nevermind. This was a dumb idea. I'll do it myself."

I start to walk away, and then I take another look at Dollhouse's absentee mother, the gorgeous blonde broad in the lavender bikini who looks like she's under enough anesthetic to receive open-heart surgery. I suddenly feel a teensy bit bad for this clingy little monster.

I turn back to Doll Haus. "I'll sign us up and eat *one* hot dog. Ya hear me? But only if you pull this thing off."

"No. How can I trust you? You already said this once before. Fool you once, shame on me. Fool you twice…"

"That's *not* the sayin', twerp." I shake my head and choke back the expletives that are bubblin' to the edges of my lips. She's a smart kid. And she's right.

I *was* plannin' to renege again.

Ah, fudgecicle.

"Come." I pat my thigh and turn around.

"I'm not some dumb poodle, you know. You can't just treat me like a dog," she nags, barely audible over the Commodores song that just started.

I ignore her canine comment and march over to the sign-up booth. I force a weak smile at the woman behind the desk. "Yeah, my granddaughter and I'd like to sign up for your silly little hot dog eatin' contest."

"Great!" she exclaims, spinnin' the sign-up sheet toward me and offerin' a pen. "Just fill this out, and I'll grab you both some liability waivers. All contestants will get their number and participation T-shirt at *You're the Wurst Grille* on Sunday before the eat-off."

"Copy that." I glare at the kid the entire time I scribble my name. Then, I slam it down on the paper and motion for her to hurry up and sign it, too.

Two legal forms later, Dolly is followin' me back through the crowd. She's excited now.

"Okay, what's the dealio? What're we doing? What's the plan, Stan?"

I beeline for an island of condiments and napkins near one of the ends of the buffet. I grab three ketchup packets, stack them neatly, and shred the top corner off all three simultaneously.

"Whoa, cool. Surprised your dentures could handle all that."

I stuff the packets in her palm. "How good are you at actin'?"

Dolly flashes a cocky smirk and backs up. Her smile morphs into a convincin' frown, and her tone comes out as a horrific cry. "Help!" She points at me accusingly. "Stranger danger! Stranger danger!" A real tear falls from her eye.

I look around, nervous at the nearby people whose attention we now have. "Uh, she's playin'. Tell them you're playin', Dollhouse."

Dolly skitters backward, her cries gettin' louder. "Please! Somebody!" The drama is cranked to maximum. A man stops stuffin' his face with his Moo Burger and rises from his chair.

"Do you need help?" He looks genuinely concerned at Dolly and glares at me like I'm a monster.

Dolly giggles, loud and maniacal. "Aaaaaand scene!" Her expression is happy again and she takes a deep bow, ketchup packets held high.

"That's not funny, kid." The man seems ticked off. "That's not something you should joke about. You could get someone in a lot of trouble!" Then, he turns his anger to me. "You need to get control of your grandkid, ma'am."

"Yeah, sure thing," I say, thinkin' it might be the only thing that'll shut this guy up. I motion for Dolly to follow me, and I roll my eyes so hard I feel like I'm gonna have retinal damage.

She follows me around the pool, and once we're in an area away from everyone, I point to Cooper Nagilnick, who is now doing the Macarena with three old ladies in purple hats and red, one-piece swimsuits. "See that guy over there?"

"Who, *Samwise Gamgee*e?"

I laugh at the Tolkien reference and then reel it in. I don't need this kid thinking she's actually funny. She's cocky enough. "I want to talk to him alone."

"Is this about Lawrence?"

I just stare at her.

She gasps. "Oh my God, are you launching an investigation? I'm in. I'm totally in. I've been thinking a lot about this, actually. I've been thinking it might be that photographer who took the picture of us this morning. Lawrence was just, like, *staring* at her the whole night at karaoke. It was so creepy!"

"No. I already talked to Jenny. She had an alibi. She's got timestamped pictures from around that time. Talkin' to her gave me a few other ideas, though. And she named Frodo over there as possibly havin' motive."

"So how do I come in?"

"I don't wanna be chasin' him around this boat all day just to see if I can squeeze in a chance to talk to him. If I waste too much time, I won't get this resolved with enough time to get karaoke up and runnin' again before the trip is over."

"Wow, you must *really* like to sing."

I scan my surroundings. "Kid, you have no idea."

Dolly looks around, too. Then, she glances up at me. "I'm in, but *only* if you let me help with the investigation."

I bark out a laugh. "Ha! Doubtful."

"Come on!"

"Don't push me, kid."

She huffs, irritated. "What do you want me to do? How are we supposed to get this guy away during the Macarena? This is the dance awkward white guys like him live for. This is his time to shine."

I point to the ketchup packets in her hand. "We're gon' walk past, and you're gonna pretend to fall and fake an injury. Palm those. Slap them against your leg and play like you scraped it. He'll have no choice but to lead us toward an infirmary. Once I get him alone, I'll hit him with my questions."

"Got it." Dolly nods with confidence and walks off in the direction of Cooper, condiments in hand. I follow behind, weavin' through intoxicated dancers.

As we get close, Devin swings around and clocks Dolly right in the face with his drink. The kid goes skiddin'.

Uh oh. That was not the plan. Klutzy-McGee might have *actually* injured her.

Dolly lands knee-first on the ground and skids along the planks. Devin scrambles to help her up, splashin' his drink down her back as he does. Dolly seethes, glarin' up at him like he's gon' be the next victim aboard this cruise ship.

Cooper breaks from his Latino line dance to check on Dolly. "Are you okay?"

Dolly remembers the plan and starts to cry, smearin' ketchup on her knee. She winces and howls, and Cooper sees the blood and nearly stumbles backward. He and Devin help her up by the armpits, and she clings to the empty condiment packets for dear life.

I come waddlin' up. "Dolly! Are you alright?" I glare at Devin, too. "Come on, *Cher*. Let's get you to a medic station." I look at Cooper. "Would you be a dear and walk us to the closest one?"

"Of course," Cooper says, panicked. He pulls his walkie off the back pocket of his shorts and mutters something into it, no doubt callin' for someone to fill in for him at the dance party.

Cosmo leans down to talk to Dolly. "You okay? That looked like a nasty spill."

Dolly is still fake cryin', although as hard as she smacked her knee, I'd probably be *really* cryin', if it were me.

"We're gon' take her to get her all bandaged up," I say.

Without another word, Cosmo scoops the girl up in his arms. She looks tiny there, like one of his spaniels back in Killjoy. It reminds me of a time he played a fireman in the background of this action movie about an oil rig fire. He did this stunt where there was an explosion, and he had to dive off the rig into the Gulf below. I must have watched that scene twenty times just for his wordless role in it.

"Lead the way," he says, and Cooper waves him through the crowd.

Minutes later, down a maze of corridors, we arrive at a nurse's station tucked away on the Lido deck. As Cosmo takes Dolly inside, I ask Cooper to hang out in the hall with me for a minute. He agrees. We watch the nurse clean Dolly up through the crack in the door, no doubt askin' if she wants any mustard or mayo to go with all that ketchup.

"Look, I know you're busy, but would you mind if I asked you a few questions?"

"Sure," he says, as if I'm about to ask him what time tomorrow's art auction is. "But for show times and events, you can always go to the Oshannic app on your phone. And to schedule an excursion, the crew at the concierge desk can book any of the exciting port activities for you."

"No, this is about Lawrence."

Cooper's expression goes as blank as a robot's.

"I know you had beef with him. And now he's dead."

"Who told you that?" He seems defensive already.

"A little birdie told me you got Lawrence hired on a few months back, and he's been makin' waves in just about every department ever since."

"Lawrence and I have been friends for years. I've known him a decade, at least."

"You don't seem too broken up over his murder." It comes out in a more accusatory tone than I'd intended, but I stand by my direct approach.

I glance through the cracked door and see Cosmo's eyes locked on me. He looks disappointed, like he's just figured out this was all a ruse. He's not wrong. It's like the man has a built-in B.S. detector.

"Ma'am, I have a job to do. I'm the Funtivities Director, not the Director of Mourning, okay? I have to slap on a happy face for these people. It's my job."

"Word around the deck is that you were gettin' real fed up with his antics."

"That's not a crime."

"Where were you around one p.m. today?"

"Oh, I need an alibi now?"

"Don't avoid the question."

He sounds annoyed. "I was hosting the *limbo*. Here. On this deck, actually."

"Got any proof of that?"

"Actually, I *do*, if you must know." He digs his phone out of his pocket. He presses the icon for a social media app and clicks on his home page. He scrolls down through a mess of color-saturated cruise photos to one where he's holdin' a limbo stick. He clicks to enlarge it. He shoves his phone into my hands, and I notice he's got an ugly little tattoo on his wrist. I can't tell if it's a dragonfly or an airplane, the line work is so bad. All I know is, even if that thing was *free*, he overpaid. "Posted at 1:12 p.m," he says smugly.

The picture is a wide-angle shot. Cooper's in a large crowd. The lens must really distort things because the arm holdin' out the camera looks long. Behind his dark sunglasses, he has a cheesy smile plastered on his face. There is a crowd of lotion-slathered people all around him. I scroll past the photo to the caption.

Sure enough. Posted at 1:12. Right in the window of time Rinalto said the murder took place.

Fudgecicle.

"We have to post a certain number of pictures throughout the day on the ship's social media page to engage with the younger crowd," Cooper explains.

"Yeah, I know." I hand his phone back.

I'm back to square one again.

"Anyone else have a beef with Lawrence?"

Nagilnick leans back against the hallway wall, his arms folded. "I don't know. Maybe Marvin. He's a bartender that works at some of the clubs around the ship."

"Does he work at *Gills*? The swim-up bar?"

Cooper nods.

"Yeah, I know him. Guy makes a mean mojito." I think for a second. "Why Marvin? What's *his* problem with Lawrence?"

"Nobody liked Lawrence. He rubbed everyone the wrong way. Half this ship was ready to throw the man overboard. Heck, we were best friends a long time ago, and he was even grating on *me*. But rumblings around the ship are that he was stabbed with a selfie-stick. Marvin is obsessed with his own image. He came out here from LA hoping to land his big break, knowing we get producers and talent scouts coming through from time to time. He's been trying to beef up his portfolio and social media following. The guy is always taking pictures."

"Yeah, he took one of us earlier for the Oshannic page."

"Did he use his selfie stick for it?"

"No."

Cooper's eyes widen. He leans in close. "It's because he 'lost' it recently." He looks at me like I'm supposed to connect the dots. "Imagine that. What a *coincidence*."

With Marvin's devilishly handsome looks, I don't doubt that he's the kind of guy who would own every camera accessory known to man. And come to think of it, he didn't take our photo with one.

The door opens, and Cosmo eases Dolly through it.

"Once they cleaned all the ketchup off, they said Dolly here only needed a Band-Aid." Cosmo's tone says he knows who was behind the condiment fake-out. Dolly gives me a subtle shrug, and I know she didn't rat me out.

"Ketchup? Cooper shakes his head, slides his phone out of my hand, and steps back. "I don't want to know. Now, if you'll excuse me, I have a dance party to host."

In a flash, he's headed back through the maze.

Cosmo finally says, "Uma Mae, may I have a word with you in private?"

Oh boy.

13

"Uma, what in God's good name are you wrapped up in now?" Cosmo asks, pullin' me inside the *Seacuterie Snack Bar* for some privacy.

"What can I get you?" A helpful woman behind the counter asks as she hops to the register.

"Gimme one'a them Scottish bagels with the lox, Sugar," I say.

"Sure thing."

I look at Cosmo. "You want one?"

Cosmo isn't findin' my antics charming right now. "Uma. It's almost nine o'clock at night, and I pulled ya in here to talk, not carbo load."

"The internet said their lox bagels are amazin'. They have a salmon-and-dill infused *schmear,* and they do the capers and red onions, the whole nine."

"I didn't pull you aside to talk *capers*, Uma Mae."

"One can eat and talk at the same time, *Cher*. Those things aren't mutually exclusive." I stare out the glass door at Dolly, who has rejoined the crowd of dancers but is still watching me out of the corner of her eye like she can read our lips. "Live a little."

"Are you wrapped up in somethin' funny again?"

"Kinda." I shrug and glance at the pink cream cheese they're smearin' on my everything bagel. My tongue sparks just thinkin' about that smoked salmon.

"What do you mean, kinda?"

"Depends on what you mean by funny."

"I think you know what I mean." His blue eyes flash at me.

I sigh. "Okay, so... There was a murder."

Cosmo rolls his neck. "Dear Lord, Uma. How do you keep finding yourself in the middle of macabre nonsense?"

"It's not like I sought this mess out."

He gives me a look that says he doesn't believe me for even one second. "Who?"

"Who what?"

"Who was killed?"

"The karaoke host, Lawrence. The staff had to question me because, you know, we kinda got into a little bit of a kerfuffle last night."

He moans, "Oh my God. Uma!"

"He wouldn't let me sing, Cosmo! Me *or* Devin. He just passed us over."

He looks around for a moment, taut jaw more defined than normal. "Who do they think did it?"

"Originally, they thought it was me."

"What? Why?"

"Because we found the body, Cosmo. That monstrous little elementary-schooler and I stumbled upon his body in the lounge this mornin' when I went to go apologize for yellin' at him last night. Someone had run that man's chest clean through with one'a them selfie sticks!"

Cosmo shakes his head. The look of disappointment he gives me says more'n his mouth ever could. Finally, he speaks. "So, did they clear you officially?"

"Not *formally*, yet. But, I mean, Dolly and I got our picture taken elsewhere while the guy was in there bleedin' all over the floor. Plus, they got security cameras, so I'm sure when they reviewed the footage, they knew the kid and I weren't in there yet."

"So why're you plantin' ketchup squibs on a minor and interrogatin' the guy leading the electric slide?"

"It was the *Macarena*." Suddenly, I panic. "Aw, man! Did I miss the electric slide?!"

"Yes."

"That's the only dance I know how to doggone do!" I shake my head. The lady behind the counter hoists my bagel up into the air. It's piled high with a mountain of pink salmon and my mouth waters. I take it from her. "Thank ya kindly, *Cher*."

"I don't believe this," Cosmo mumbles quietly.

"I was interrogatin' that little Hobbit fella because one of the broads who takes the cruise pictures said he was once real good friends with Lawrence. I guess lately he's been upset with the guy for gettin' in trouble. Apparently, he gets obsessive with some of the girls on the ship, and they've had to give him warnings and such about his skeevy behavior."

"Uma, this isn't your case to meddle in. You put yourself in harm's way the last time, and Carl's killer nearly put you in the ground, too! Look around, darlin'. You're on a boat at sea on a gorgeous night with your family and friends. Don't squander your relaxing vacation on some quest for justice."

"I don't care about justice, Cosmo! I want karaoke! As long as there's an investigation goin' on, they got the karaoke lounge closed off and ain't no one singin'!"

"Uma Mae Blanchard, it is my solemn vow to you that if you drop this nonsense right now, I will take you to the finest bar in all of southern Lose-yanna when we get back to port."

I take a bite of the bagel and moan. With a mouthful of salmon and bread, I ask, "You sure you don't want one of these? They're divine!"

Cosmo looks down at it but doesn't dignify my silly question with an answer. "I'm going to go out there and enjoy my night." He leans down and plants a kiss on the crown of my head. Then, he says, "I suggest you do the same."

Cosmo walks out the door, and Dolly rushes in.

"Was he giving you a lecture?"

I nod. "He's probably right. I'm squanderin' my vacation on this nonsense."

"Hmmm." Dolly swishes her hip out. "Never pegged you for a quitter."

Then, she leaves. Just as she disappears in the crowd behind Devin, I see a large man in a pressed, black uniform drift through the crowd. Rinalto Nunca's chrome dome shines in the colored dance party lights as he cruises 'round the deck like a shark, lurkin', lookin' for easy prey.

I slink out the side door of *Seacuterie* before Rinalto can spot me through the glass. I take the remainder of my bagel back to my stateroom so I can eat in peace.

14

"Uma, can I join you for breakfast?" Dolly asks, runnin' a hand along the linen tablecloth beside me. My family looks at her.

"Where's your mother?" I ask. The look on Dolly's silent face tells me the woman is probably still in bed, sleepin' one off.

After a moment, I sigh and point at the empty chair between my grandsons at the end of the table. "Fine. But you're sittin' on the kiddie side."

I look at the rest of my tablemates. "Everyone, this is Dolly. Dolly, this is everyone."

She waves. It's the first time I've seen her act shy. "Hi, everyone."

"Go on. Sit." I motion with my head.

"Uh, how do you two know each other?" Daniel asks.

I point my butter knife at him. "You ever go to Scotch tape somethin', and you get the frickin' tape stuck to the end of your finger? You go to get it off, and then it just gets stuck to your *other* finger?" I point the knife at her. "Meet Scotch tape."

Daniel takes it all in and then goes back to eatin' his steak and eggs.

"Honey, do you want some pancakes or waffles?" Jane asks her.

"No, thank you. Saving myself for lunch." Dolly flashes me some violent-lookin' eyes, and I suddenly remember that today is the day of the stupid hot dog eatin' competition.

I set my forkful of blueberry waffle back down on the plate and turn to look at Devin. "You were all over the place last night."

"Was I?" Devin looks alarmed.

"You clocked Dolly with your coconut on the dance floor."

"Sorry," he mumbles to her, embarrassed.

"Then, at the end of the night, when I left the bagel place, I saw you arguin' with some scrawny guy who was wearin' half of your newest cocktail."

He holds his head. "Dear God, I don't remember *any* of that."

"What's the last thing you *do* remember?"

"I remember going to some honor the veteran's thing. I saw Cosmo there."

I look at the two empty seats where Cosmo and his daughter should be. They must've decided to have breakfast elsewhere this mornin'. Or maybe they slept in.

I hear Dolly suddenly cry out, "Ow! Stop it!"

"Hey, hey, hey! Stop that!" Daniel barks at his children. "Let her go! Stop trying to cut her hair, Stokely. Put the knife down and eat your pancakes."

Duncan laughs, and Dolly glares over at me like she's been banished to purgatory.

"The veteran's thing was early afternoon, around three o'clock, right? I meant to go to it but ended up bein' interrogated by the doggone boat police."

"What?!" Jane says with a gasp.

I wave her away. "Long story. Don't worry about it." I turn back to Devin. "What do you remember other'n that?"

"Not much. I was trying to stave off the hangover from the night before with a little hair of the dog, but then I figured I'm on vacation, and this booze pass makes the most financial sense if you get a stiff drink every ninety minutes. So I just kept setting timers on my phone and… The rest of the day's a blur."

"Where were you 'round one o'clock?" I narrow my eyes and flash Dolly a look that tells her to pay attention to his answer.

Devin shrugs. "No clue. I have lost all sense of time since I boarded this ship." He points to his bare wrist. "I took off my watch somewhere. Oh well."

"You don't seem like you're a stranger to bein' blackout drunk."

He laughs. "Not the first time. Won't be the last, I'm sure." I can see in his heavily-lidded eyes that he's already quite hammered.

"You ever get violent when you're blackout drunk, Devin?"

Suddenly, I remember him tryin' to lunge at Lawrence over gettin' passed up for our duet.

Devin's smile fades. Then, he nods. "A couple of times I've heard I've caused a stir."

"I see," I say, starin' right into Dolly's eyes. She nods as if she understands me fully.

Suddenly, Devin's laugh rings out over the otherwise-silent table. "Plus, there was the time I got drunk and..."

Devin falls silent and he lowers his head. We all watch him in suspense as his head bobs. I can't tell if he is laughin' or cryin'. Finally, he looks up, red eyes brimmin' with tears. He throws his napkin on the remains of his breakfast, scoots his chair out with a loud groan, and walks off without another word.

15

Day 3 - *11:55 am*
You're the Wurst Grille
Lido Deck 9

"Here is your number," a man in a white uniform with a *You're the Wurst Grille* lanyard says to me as he pins a fabric number to my souvenir shirt. It says, *I gobbled dogs with the best* alongside a drawn-on woman's face, cheeks stuffed with food.

"What's the number to beat?" Dolly asks, beaming.

"You just have to eat more than the others around you to win the golden buns trophy," he says.

"I mean, what's the current high score?" she asks.

"Oh, honey, you don't have to beat that number. I think it's something like," he makes a grotesque face, "twenty-nine dogs."

"Buns, too?"

"Yes, buns, too."

Dolly nods like the challenge is accepted. Then, she looks up at me and rubs her palms together like a cartoon villain. "I'm starving. This is gonna be cake."

I roll my eyes. "If your mom ends up suin' me over this, I'm never talkin' to you again."

"She'd have to be *conscious* to sue you." Dolly looks out at the gathered crowd.

"Good luck," Cooper says to Dolly.

"I don't need luck. I got the *hunger*," Dolly replies, eyes narrowing in agitation. Then, she looks at one of the other competitors standin' beside her, a man in his forties with a rather rotund figure and a nametag that says Spencer. She lunges a little like she's going to start a fight with an adult twice as tall as her. "What? You think you can beat me? Bring it on. I'll mop the floor with you!"

There is something feral *about that child...*

"Relax, psycho." I pull her back by the shoulder. Then, I look up at the man she just threatened. "Sorry. Might be best to give her a wide berth until we can put her muzzle back on."

Cooper Nagilnick walks into the grille, microphone in hand. He covers it and whispers to the five of us, "Who's ready to gobble some doggies?"

Dolly lets out a Rick Flair-type "Woooooooo!" and the rest of us offer a very lackluster golf clap. We all follow Cooper out to a long table on the stage filled with plate-upon-plate of hot dogs in untoasted buns. We all take our seats. Cooper gets the crowd riled with his little spiel and introduces us all from a note on his phone. "Give it up for Spencer, Alan, Heather, Dolly, and Umaaaaaaa!"

The crowd goes surprisingly wild, and one shirtless man with his gut hangin' over the band of his swim trunks lets out a series of eardrum-puncturin' whistles. I look around and see Isa in the audience. Near her stands Cosmo, lookin' more shocked than I've ever seen him.

Oh, sweet Marie Laveau, I can't be havin' that man watch me gobble weenie upon weenie like my last name is Lovelace!

I suddenly want to fake an injury or a heart attack or somethin' to get me out of here. Heck, even a *real* heart attack might be preferable to this embarrassment right now.

The Ricky Martin song gets louder. He's croonin' about baking bonbons or something. A few people on the outskirts of the crowd start dancin' with themselves. One woman busts into a full-blown cha-cha.

"I'm gonna have our contestants introduce themselves real quick." Cooper hands the mic to the portly man on the end, the one Dolly threatened mere moments ago.

Nervously, the man takes it and says, "Hi. I'm Spencer. I'm from Denver, Colorado. And I *relish* this chance to eat a lot of hot dogs!"

I roll my eyes at the pun. The crowd cheers, and Spencer passes the mic down.

"Hi, I'm Alan. I'm a banker from Atlanta. Go Bulldogs!"

That makes a few people in the crowd cheer and boo at the same time.

"If I fall behind, I just hope I can *ketchup* to you all." He laughs at his own attempt at a joke while looking around. He passes the mic down.

"I'm Heather. I'm an author from Casper, Wyoming. My Pitt Bulls and I just love the snow up there. I guess you could say that I'm used to my fair share of... *chili dogs*." She does a little carefree dance in her seat. "I'm ready to become more nitrate than human! I will be your new reigning champion and will be going home with golden buns if it's the last thing I do."

"Me, too!" some lady in the crowd screams, then shakes her rump toward the stage.

Heather, the stunnin' brunette, hands the mic to Dolly and pounds her fists on the table. Everyone cheers.

Dolly presses the mic to her lips the same way kids put their mouths too close to one'a them gross water fountain nozzles. "My name is Dorothy. I *hate* the Wizard of Oz. And I don't think I'm in Wichita, Kansas any more, Toto."

The crowd is hyped, and the whistler deafens us all again, following it with a "You go, Dorothy!"

Dolly tosses the mic rudely on the paper plate in front of me. I pick it up. Best to get this over with.

"My name is Uma. I'm from Killjoy, Lose-yanna, and I hate puns. Thank you." I start to put the mic down, and then I pick it back up again and look at Nagilnick. "Are these Hebrew Nationals?" I pull a limp hot dog from its bun and waggle it at Cooper. "Can I at least get some ketchup or somethin'?"

He takes the microphone back from me to answer. "Oooh, I'm sorry. No condiments allowed, I'm afraid." He turns back to the crowd. "Are we ready?!"

They howl and cheer. Cosmo smiles at me while he claps.

"On your marks! Get set! Gobble those dogs!" He points to the girl at the nearby kiosk, and she presses a button, startin' a lively Gloria Estefan song. As the music pours through the speakers, the other contestants start crammin' the dogs in their gullets. I grab a meat-cicle at one-tenth of the speed that they do and start to nibble the end of it, tryin' to force myself to smile like I'm not bein' forced into this stupid contest.

Next to me, Dolly is washin' down her second hot dog and bun with a sip of water. She looks like a hamster with her cheeks full like that.

I see Jenny Applebaum in the back of the crowd, snappin' pictures of the event with her big, black camera. She glances to her left and makes eye contact with someone, flittin' her fingers in a flirty little wave. Then, she blows a kiss. I wonder if Drew Pye is bringin' her another boba tea, but I don't see him around anywhere. I only see former competitive eatin' champs in judges' chairs, a gaggle of onlookers, and a bunch of kids splashin' 'round in the pool with the swim-up bar.

My nosy spyin' is interrupted by the sound of Alan vomiting into one of the buckets placed below the table.

"Oh, so sorry, sir, but you are disqualified!" Cooper says into the mic while pattin' the man on the back. "Let's give Alan a round of applause."

A few people cheer like mad, obviously full of Jell-O shots and rum. I look over to see Heather soakin' one of her buns in her glass of water, determination in her eyes.

Several minutes pass, and I finally finish my second dog. I would have stopped at one, but they're actually not half bad. Still, I wanted to remain at least a *little* ladylike in the presence of Cosmo.

"And that is time, folks! Dogs down, please!" Cooper says into the microphone.

Everyone leans back in their chair, miserable or hurtin' except Dolly and I. Dolly throws the bun in her hand angrily at the table and, with a mouthful of meat, she growls somethin' that sounds like, "Not fair!"

"Chill out, kid," I grumble in her ear.

"Alan was disqualified. Let's give it up for Alan one more time!"

The crowd cheers again.

"Alright, judges? How did they do?" Cooper smiles like a game show host.

The judges confer. The one in the middle finally takes the microphone they share. He says, "Well, Uma came in fourth with two hot dogs."

The crowd boos me. Cosmo claps and then gives me two 'thumbs-up.'

"Heather came in third place with nine hot dogs."

Heather shrugs and says, "I tried!"

"And the winner by one whole hot dog…" The judge extends his arm. "Spencer!"

The crowd roars, and Gloria Estefan comes back on. Dolly shoves the plate of remainin' dogs real hard. It nearly falls off the front of the table and onto some of the day-drinkin' dancers below.

"Don't be a poor sport, kid," I growl.

"I lost by one dog!"

"Spencer, here you go," Cooper shouts as he hands the man a trophy made of gold plastic in the shape of a hot dog. "You earned it."

Cooper hands Dolly a runner-up sash. She snatches it from him, still poutin'. Then, she looks at me. "I am *not* wearing this!"

16

"How are you feelin'?" I ask as the toilet in the stall nearby flushes.

"Well, most of the hot dogs are washing out to sea right about now," Dolly says, voice frail. She exits the stall, her face white as the ghost I once saw in the upstairs window of the Nottoway Plantation, a few years before it done burned down.

"Feel better now that you upchucked?"

She nods.

"Good. Wash your face, heathen. I'll buy you a consolation smoothie. Maybe it'll help settle your stomach."

"I can't believe I lost by *one* hot dog. This sucks!" She pulls her sash out of the back pocket of her shorts and jams it in the bathroom's trash can.

"Eh. Let that guy enjoy the win," I say as Dolly blots her face and washes her tremblin' hands. "You saw the guy. That's probably the best thing that's happened in his life. You have your whole existence ahead of you for better achievements. Plus… That poor sap was from *Denver*."

"So?"

"So? He's got an unfair advantage. Mary Jane is legal up there. Guy probably came to the contest with the munchies. When those hit, you'll eat the sidin' off a house."

"What's Mary Jane?"

"Oh, come on, don't make me spell it out for ya."

"I'm serious. I don't know what that is."

"The *devil's lettuce*?"

She just stares at me like I've grown a third eye.

"You mean to tell me you know what *Taxi Driver* is, but not marijuana?"

"Ohhhhhhh, you mean, like, weed?"

I whisper. "*Shhhh! Yes, like weed.*"

"Why didn't you just call it that? Who the heck calls it 'Mary Jane' or the 'devil's lettuce'?" She scoffs. "Besides, I don't think you can bring weed on a cruise ship." She wipes her hands, wads the paper, and makes a basket from all the way across the bathroom.

"Smokin' on planes is illegal, too. Didn't stop me from smokin' half a pack of American Spirits in the crapper on the way to Newark."

"Menthols or regulars?"

"How do you…?" I follow her out into the shop.

"I smoked a menthol once. My friend Kim stole one off her stepdad and brought it to school."

"I see." I honestly don't know what to say to that. "You know you shouldn't smoke, right?"

"You literally just said you smoke. Illegally, too."

"Don't use me as your role model, kid. That's just a disaster waitin' to happen." I shove Dolly playfully by the head toward the counter. "Go on. Order somethin'. On me."

She examines the menu. Then, she looks at me. "Will you get one, too? These look *weird*."

"That photographer broad, Jenny, swears by this boba stuff." I shrug. "Eh, what the heck. Why not?" I look at the lady behind the register and hand her my lanyard. "What's the best one'a them little loogie-ball drinks you got?"

"You mean the tapioca pearls? My favorite is the avocado boba."

"Are you prankin' me?"

"No, ma'am. It tastes much better than it sounds. It's milk, avocado, and your choice of sweetener. Or if you have a sweet tooth, I also recommend the mango bubble milk tea. It's really sweet, but hits just right on a hot day like today."

"Yeah… Gimme one of those mango ones, would ya?"

"And for her?" the lady asks.

Dolly steps up to the register. "I'll do the jasmine smoothie with the purple popping bobas."

"Gross." I look down at Dolly and find myself smilin'. It feels like only yesterday my own girls were her age.

The lady hands me my lanyard back and smiles. "They'll be ready in a flash."

***

"How's yours?" I ask, embarrassed that mine is already one-third gone by the time we settle into two open teal-blue reclinin' loungers up on the Lido Deck.

Dolly slams the butt of her palm against her forehead. "So good." Then, in a high, squeaky pitch, she hollers, *"Brain freeze!"*

"Well, slow down. Ain't no one takin' it from ya."

I lean back in my lounge chair, feelin' the warmth of the beatin' sun crisp me like a *graton*.

Dolly shields her eyes from the sun and looks around at all the people in various stages of their sunny, poolside adventures. "So, who do you think could have done it, Uma?"

"You mean…?"

"Iced the karaoke jerk."

"Well, I had a feelin' it was Jenny just 'cause of her proximity to the body there for a while, but I believe her alibi. I can't really argue with timestamped pictures. And for that same reason, I'm countin' Cooper out, too."

"The Funtivities guy? Why'd you think it was Cooper in the first place?"

"I asked Jenny who had a problem with Lawrence. She said everybody. But Cooper apparently got the guy hired and was gettin' tired of having Lawrence's bad behavior reflect on him."

"Where was he when Lawrence was murdered?"

"Showed me a picture of him hostin' the limbo party on the social media page right around that time."

"Hmmmm."

"Then there was Marvin, the bartender at the swim-up bar. He didn't seem to be too broken up over Lawrence's death."

"What about Devin?"

"Klutzy Devin?"

"You heard him at karaoke when the guy passed you over. He said he was gonna kill him."

"Yeah, I know." I stare off at the land in the distance. We must be gettin' close to the port in Cozumel. "Plus, all the songs he wanted to sing were songs about killin' people."

"And at breakfast, you saw him rush out of there like a weirdo when you brought up his blackouts."

"Yeah, and his recollection of everything seems real fuzzy because he's been drinkin' like a fish this whole cruise, so it's not like he has any kind of alibi."

"You think he is capable of murder?"

I snort. "Kid, I think anyone is capable of anything."

"I think we need to find out more about Devin and why he just rushed out of breakfast like that. What is he hiding?"

I shrug. "Beats me."

Dolly stares out at the waves for a moment. "Does he have insta?"

"Insta-what?"

"Ugh. *Gram.*" Dolly rolls her eyes and sticks out her hand. "Lemme borrow your phone. We should do some intel on our ol' pal Devin."

I reluctantly hand her my phone and go back to drinkin' my mango smoothie thingy. I suck up a boba ball. It looks like Pac Man chasin' a line of pale yella ghosts through my clear straw. When it hits the back of my throat, I nearly choke. As I explode the sugar-filled, rubbery wad between my faux molars, I shake my head. "Those things *are* tasty. But I swear I'll never get used to suckin' up ping pong balls through a hose-sized straw like this. It's delicious, but it's unsettlin'."

Dolly ignores me, still starin' at my phone. "Good Lord, the font on this thing is huge! You could see it from space."

"You'll get old too one day. Trust."

"Why don't you just wear glasses?"

"I do. Sometimes. Are you gonna harass me or search the web?"

Dolly rolls her eyes. "What's his last name?"

"Oh, Lord, I know it. He said it at dinner the other night. Co… *Co-hell-no*, I think. Somethin' like that."

"Costello?"

"Hmmm. No. I don't think so. But similar."

"Cohelo, maybe?"

"Yeah. That seems right. I dunno. Try it."

Her tiny fingers fly across the screen for a while. She could be writin' a novel in binary code for all I know. Or searchin' the dark web for something she can use to frame me with later with the FBI.

"Devin Cohelo. That's definitely him. Third one down. Looks like he's single. *Shocker*. Grip in the film industry. Seems like he mostly works on those low-budget Christmas movies with all the D-list stars."

"Oh, I love those," I say without any trace of irony.

"Gross." She scrolls on. "Oh snap! 'Rest in peace, Buddy Warren.' There's a memorial thing on his wall."

I lean over with my sweatin' plastic cup and take a peek, the blinding sun makin' it hard to make anything out.

"There are comments underneath. Someone called him a *murderer*."

"Oooh. What else does it say?"

"Let me poke around for a minute and see." She falls silent for a bit as I Hoover up some more boba wads. It's almost like a game.

"These ain't bad, actually. I have half a mind to try that avocado one she was talkin' about." I look over at Dolly's drink, and it's empty.

Dolly's eyes go wide. She flips the phone toward me, and I squint to see the tiny image. "He's got a picture of him on the set of some military Christmas movie. Aha! And what's *that*?"

She points to a diagonal line at the bottom. I shrug. I can barely see the doggone picture, much less make out what the line is. "Dunno. Enlighten me."

Dolly looks at me like I'm a moron. "It's a selfie stick. A tiny little bit of one."

"Hmmm."

"And have you seen Devin take any pictures on this cruise with a selfie stick?"

"No."

"Maybe that's because it's jammed in Lawrence's chest!"

She leans back and scrolls through more of his social media for a bit as our ship prepares to dock at Puerta Maya, the cruise port in Cozumel. I see a forest of Bird of Paradise plants linin' beaches of tan sand. A flock of seagulls flies overhead, wings outstretched but not flappin'. They follow our boat lookin' as though they're stationary, painted on a blue backdrop in vivid detail.

"Uma!" Dolly shoots straight up in her lounge chair, the sun reflectin' off her golden curls. "There's an article on the internet about it: *Film Worker Takes Plea Deal in*

On-Set Slaying." Dolly gasps. "It's Devin! Maybe he killed this guy, and now he's got, like, the bloodlust?"

I can't help but laugh. "The *bloodlust?*"

"I saw it in a movie once. This guy killed someone, and he got the bloodlust, and he became a serial killer!"

"I think your mom is doin' you a real disservice by lettin' you watch whatever you want all the time, kid. You met the guy. He doesn't seem like he's got the lust for anythin' beyond a strong buzz."

"I'm telling you, Uma. I got a bad feeling about this guy! He friggin' spelled it out for us. He said he was gonna kill the guy… And, then, he did!"

"So, what are you sayin'? I should drop his name with security and say, 'We have a hunch. Please follow up on this?'"

Dolly thinks for a minute. "We need a taped confession."

"Calm down, *Serpico*. I left my cassette recorder at home."

She groans. "What are you? A hundred-and-ten? Who uses a cassette recorder anymore? Your phone has one built-in."

"Sure it does, kid."

Suddenly, I hear my voice playin' back to me through my own phone.

"Sure it does, kid."

Dolly holds the cell up with a smug look of satisfaction. "See?! You gotta get a confession on here for the FBI!"

"I don't have to do nothin' but die and pay taxes, Dollhouse."

"Do you want a murderer running around with us on this giant, floating casket? *If he's got the bloodlust…*"

"There ain't no such thing as bloodlust, kid!" I swipe at her and snatch my phone outta her hand. I look around, thinkin' for a second.

Maybe the twerp has a point. I offer my phone back to her. "Okay. You win. Show me how to record with this blasted thing."

17

I make my way down the gangway and through the duty-free mall. The Cozumel port is bustlin' with tourists clad in sloppy summer-wear. The air smells like coconut sunscreen and saltwater.

"Where to, first?" Dolly asks, her voice risin' from hip-height.

"I don't know where *you're* goin', kid, but it sure ain't with me. You're on your own here. I told you to stay on the boat."

"Are you insane?"

"I'm goin' shoppin' and then I'mma sit my big ol' butt down at that restaurant over yonder," I point to a low building with a terracotta roof and a huge courtyard full of tables. "Then, I am gon' finish out this port day by ingestin' about five thousand calories' worth of Bloody Marys and authentic Mexican guacamole before I drunkenly waddle my behind back on up that gangway this evenin'." I scoff.

"Sounds good. I'm in."

I halt in my tracks and turn to her. "Dolly, no. I'm puttin' my foot down. I am not gon' be responsible for watchin' you in some foreign country. That's *not* happenin'. Heck, I ain't even doin' that for my *real* family, and some of them are around here doin' God-knows-what."

Without another word, Dolly storms off ahead of me on the gangway, her light-up shoes splashin' the salt-encrusted planks with various colors. Eventually, she makes it outta sight, blendin' in with the throng of people milling around the flea market-style shops full of marked-up Mexican wares.

I browse the windows at the upscale duty-free diamond store and meander through the corn-husk-lined artisan stalls with tables chock-full of cheap wooden maracas, colorful handcrafted dolls, Mexican candies, flutes, puppets, and straw hats. I see a pile of bright, shiny *luchador* masks that look like somethin' Duncan and Stokely would love to wrestle around the front yard in. I am tryin' one on (for the heck of it) when, out of the corner of one of the eye holes, I see Devin waltz by. He is lookin' around suspiciously, and he has a rumpled plastic bag in his hand. He glances around. He looks like he suspects somebody is followin' him.

Wouldn't want to disappoint, now would I?

I should follow. See what he's up to. See if I can get a confession.

"Uh, *quanto* for *el masko*?" I ask the lady workin' the stall while pointin' at the gleaming fire engine-red mask I'm wearin'. Its silver embellishments reflect the sun back on her cherubic face.

"*Quince dolores.*"

"Uh, gimme *dos, por favor.*" I hand her thirty bucks, and she pretends to smile as I snatch up a shamrock green mask, too, and stuff it in my beach bag.

"Looks good," she manages in English while givin' me a thumbs up.

"*Gracias,*" I say before I flee the stall, followin' Devin toward town, givin' him a wide berth.

I strip off the mask just as Devin enters a building with a sign that says something in Spanish with the giant words SCOOTER RENTALS beneath it. I slink in through the side door and keep my body turned away from him once we're inside. At one register, I hear him ask to rent a Moped.

God, I haven't been on a two-wheeled vehicle in ages. Might be a fun way to see the city.

…And to see where Devin is scurryin' off to.

Maybe he's gonna dump some evidence. I wonder what's in the bag? A blood-stained shirt? A broken piece of a selfie stick? Lawrence's missin' cell phone?

"We have thirty-minute or ninety-minute rentals, sir," one of the middle-aged Latino men behind the counter says to Devin.

"*Treinta, por favor, mi amigo,*" Devin replies.

"*Si, Señor.*" The man presses some paperwork toward him, and he signs it blindly. "*Gracias.*"

"*De nada.*"

"300 pesos, *por favor.*"

300 pesos?

Heck, that's like… less than twenty bucks!

I wave down the other worker and slide a crisp twenty across the counter at him. "*Un* scooter, *por favor.* Thirty *minutos.*"

The man nods and gives me a similar form. I work hard to turn my back to Devin as I scribble down my name. I could be signin' away rights to my firstborn for all I know. I shove the paper back at the man and both workers disappear into the back.

In the reflection of one of the windows, I see Devin walk over to a row of colorful scooters. He grabs the handlebars, and the weight swings more than he anticipated. It topples against the next scooter, which topples into the *next,* and they all tumble to the floor like well-placed dominoes.

Devin swears, and one of the men comes rushin' out of the back with a set of keys in his hand. He rushes over to the mess of vehicles on the floor and starts to pick 'em up.

***

Ten minutes later, I'm purring down the road on an off-brand Mexican economy scooter with the wind whistlin' through the holes in my red *luchador* mask. I am tryin' to stay a safe distance behind Devin, but that is provin' to be one of the hardest feats of my life for a combination of reasons. The kid keeps speedin' up and slowin' down. The road is riddled with more potholes than Nawlins -- *if you can believe that!* Not to mention, stray dogs keep gallopin' out of the brush and scrub, darting out from behind cacti into the road in front of us. I've nearly wiped out three separate times already.

I cruise through the city of Cozumel, relishing the sights. This is not a way I ever imagined seein' this place, whizzin' through the streets on 49-ccs of pure fun. The homes I pass are humble, many without windows, some with their doors wide open even in this incredible heat. I pass a family sittin' in their yard, hand-rolling flour tortillas beneath the shade of a blanket pinned up on clotheslines overhead. With every quarter of a mile I ride, the scooter's pumpkin-orange fairing collects the splattered corpses of twenty or so more bugs. It's starting to resemble a Jackson Pollock painting.

The ride is long and curvy, and my scooter sputters at a sign that says: ALTO. I start to wonder if I might get stranded out here in the middle of Cozumel.

Or worse.

If Devin's killed at least twice, it just *now* finally occurs to me that I might be victim number three! He could stab me out here in the middle of nowhere and roll me in a ditch behind some agave, and no one'll find me until I start to bloat.

With the image of my hot, rottin' corpse in the forefront of my mind, I decide to give him a little more room to roam up ahead. If I lose him, so be it.

Just as I let off the accelerator, I see another stray dog dart out of the brush, spooked by the sound of Devin's scooter engine, which sounds like a mix between my new neighbor's gas-powered weed-eater and extended flatulence.

The canine shoots out in front of Devin's front tire. To avoid hittin' it, he jerks on the handlebars with a swift motion and over-corrects. The dog yips in fear, and Devin goes shootin' off the raised dirt road!

He slams right into the ditch. I hear a crash and a scream.

I pull over by the edge of the road. Thank goodness, he's alive! He doesn't appear to be bleedin' from any major injury, but it looks like he rolled right smack into a patch of spiky cacti.

"Help!" he bellows, holdin' an outstretched arm toward me as I struggle to force the kickstand down with my dusty Mary Janes. Finally, it bites into the parched soil, and I am able to get the machine to prop on it. I hear my hip snap like a dry twig as I lift it over the back tire to dismount.

"Please, sir! For the love of God! Help me!"

"I'm not a *sir*!" I grumble. I rip off my *luchador* mask and examine the shiny material. It's speckled with dust and a bit of bird poo. I make a face at it. "I'll have you know, I'm one hundred percent woman."

"Uma?" Devin cries, confused and elated and angry, all in equal measure. He tries to pull himself off the cacti and screams bloody murder.

"Hold your horses, you clumsy flippin' pincushion! Gimme a minute to get down there! Geez-Louise! You millennials are so doggone impatient!"

"I'm *Gen-Z*," he wails.

"Kid, I don't care if you're considered pi or binary. If you don't want me to leave ya out here lookin' like the new head demon in the Hellraiser franchise, you'll shut your yap!"

I surf down the side of the embankment, nearly losin' my balance as I skid. I stabilize myself just in time so I don't teeter face-first into the cactus juttin' out between Devin's spine-covered legs.

I look him over quickly, tryin' to determine the best way to pull him up without causin' more harm to the kid. Maybe it's not the worst idea to have a potential murderer owe you a favor.

I extend my hand, and he grabs it. "I'm gonna pull slow. One, because I'm goin' on seventy. Two, because I feel like this ain't the kind of situation that calls for rippin' off a Band-Aid."

He grimaces and nods. I tug him upward a little, and he screams, risin' a few slow inches at a time until he falls to the side and collapses on his palms and knees in the dirt. There are prickers all over his back, and I have to hold back a joke about how much he looks like a porcupine right now.

"What are you… doing… all the way… out here?" he asks in between small movements, until he's standing.

"Can't a woman take a scenic scooter ride in a foreign land?"

"In a *luchador* mask?"

"I didn't wanna rent a helmet, and I wanted to keep the bugs off my face." Then, I slap him upside his head lightly. "Hey, I'm not the one on trial here, anyway. Mind your own business."

"Can you…?" He points to his back, indicating that he needs me to pull all the spikes out.

I sigh. "What's in it for me?"

He looks at me, a bit appalled about the *quid pro quo*. Then, with his voice teeterin' on the edge of full-blown cryin', he finally says, "I'll buy you a stiff drink at *Tres Amigos* back at the port if you just get these out right now."

"Now we're talkin', kid!" I point to a rock nearby, one that goes up to my thighs. "Mm-kay. Go sit on that li'l boulder."

"I can't sit right now, Uma! You'd have to get the ones outta my butt first." He points to his rear end.

I groan. *He's correct. He can't rightly sit on them spikes.*

"Fine." I kneel down in the dirt, lava-hot pebbles burnin' my bony kneecaps. I start pluckin' prickers out of his backside, watchin' his fists ball up in frustration.

"Uma?"

Just as he says my name, I look over to my right to see a plastic bag, the one he'd been carryin' through the marketplace.

I can almost see inside…

I picture it full of blood-spattered clothes, and the handle of the selfie stick the ship's coroner is probably pullin' outta Lawrence right now alongside the FBI.

"Yeah?" I finally respond.

"Were you… following me?"

I start pullin' cactus spikes out of his butt faster, with less care. I wanna get this over with before I'm kneeled down so long I can't get back up again.

"No," I lie. I don't think he's buyin' it. "But you best thank your lucky stars that I ended up out here in the middle'a nowhere with you."

"Where were you headed?"

"I was just… scootin' around. Seein' the sights."

"The sights? There's not really much out this way, Uma."

Devin sounds like he's onto my nonsense.

"Honey, this ain't my first time in Cozumel. There's only so much a woman can do at that port unless she wants to bring back a suitcase fulla diamonds and duty-free booze. I figured if I rented me a scooter, I'd be able to explore this-here fine city in a whole new way. Maybe see some things I never would've imagined." I pluck two more cactus spines out of his right butt-cheek. "And boy, this trip did not disappoint."

I scan his backside again for any I might have missed.

"There, sit down on this-here rock and let me get at the rest."

He helps me up, and I groan long and loud. As he cops a squat on the craggy, tan boulder, I catch a glimpse of his overturned scooter in the spiny brush. I can't help but laugh.

"What's so funny?"

"Well, if you knew my drivin' record with vehicles with *four* wheels, you'd know that odds were in *my* favor to be the one to wreck. Not you. Maybe your clumsiness and bad luck are far more powerful forces than my own wanton recklessness behind the wheel."

I pluck an inch-and-a-half-long spine out of his back, and his howl echoes out across the dusty plain.

18

Day 3 - *4:26 pm*
Tres Amigos Bar
Cozumel Mexico Port

"Mojito. Extra mint. Top shelf rum. Oh, and it's goin' on his tab, hun." I shove a bony finger toward Devin.

The tan bartender adjusts her long, black ponytail and smiles. "*Si.*"

"*Un cervesa,*" Devin says. "Mexican blonde. Whatever you got. *Frio, por favor.* And keep 'em comin'."

"*Si,*" she says with a nod.

I settle into a wooden seat at the bar that happens to be creakier than my left knee. I look around at the colorful, folded bandannas hangin' pointy-side down like Viking flags from the wooden beams above. They offer a punch of color, as do all the banana-yellow table tops populatin' the place. The bar has no walls, and a humid gulf-bound breeze sweeps through from the marketplace, wrappin' around me

156

like a warm hug from a sweaty relative. It brings with it the cilantro-infused smell of *pico de gallo,* and suddenly I'm starvin'.

"Let's cut the crap, Uma." Devin looks exhausted, and his white T-shirt is covered in tan dust. He leans in closer, his voice low. "Why were you following me?"

"I already said—"

"Uma. Don't lie. I just wanna know why."

This is it. My time to confront him for murderin' Lawrence. At least there'll be witnesses all around if he tries to attack me.

Albeit *drunk ones.*

A wasted woman by a wooden pillar cackles, cuttin' through the tension. Then, she spins and starts dancin' on a man in a way that should frankly be illegal in public.

I look around, tryin' to mentally take in all of my available exit paths if this kid decides I need to join Lawrence in his eternal slumber. I finally decide on the water. There's a clear path to it if I throw my bar stool down as an obstacle. I'm a strong enough swimmer to buy myself some time, surely.

The bartender slams a sweaty bottle of beer on the counter in front of him and points at the man muddlin' my mint in a glass behind her. *"Un momento con tu mojito."*

"Sure thang, hun." I force a smile. *"Muchos grass-yass."*

"Spill it," Devin growls, pickin' a pricker I must have missed outta his forearm. He flicks it onto the blue-and-white tiled floor and stares at me.

"I don't know how to say this…" I eye the plate of tortilla chips and queso that one of the bartenders walks by with. I suddenly consider postponin' my accusation in an attempt to get a little food in me.

"Just say it."

My eyes meet his. "Alright. I guess I'll just come straight out with it."

"Please do."

"Your mojito," the bartender says as he sets my drink in front of me.

"Thanks." I pull out the mini umbrella and hold the paper part in my palm, toothpick point jutting out through my fingers, just in case I have to stab it into Devin to buy time to scramble away. I suck down a third of the entire drink in a long, nervous swig and groan with pleasure at how good it is. If I weren't about to get attacked by a vicious murderer right now, this'd be a moment of pure vacation bliss.

"I know you killed Lawrence." I shrug. "There. I said it."

Devin looks so confused, like he's shocked that I put it all together. "What? You think I killed that wiener?

"Yes." I suck down another third of my drink and rattle my ice noisily in my glass.

"Why on earth would you think I killed him? He was a little annoying, sure, but I'm not a cold-blooded killer."

"He wasn't your first." I squint my eyes even more, so much that I almost can't even see him anymore. "I know you've killed before."

My hand grips my mojito glass so hard that I feel like I'm gon' crush it into shards. I'm ready to bash this kid in the noggin with it if he lunges in anger. Instead, he slumps back in his chair and looks as sad as all get-out.

"I have, and I think about it every single day of my life. I will *never* be able to escape that. But it was an accident."

"Wait… what?"

"I said it was an accident!" Tears start streamin' from the outer corners of both eyes and he chugs half his beer and looks up at the bandannas in the rafters. "How'd you find out?"

"One internet search of your name turned up a whole bunch of headlines."

"So, you read the articles, right? You should know I'm not a murderer."

"Well, I," I hesitate, "I saw enough."

"So, you know it was an accident, then. They said I didn't put the pin back in the lift right when I reconnected the basket. Then, when I jerked the controls…" His hand comes up, and his claw-like fist mimics the crashin' down of something. "He shouldn't have been standing under the basket, Uma! We were wrapped on set for the day! He should have been leaving to go home. Why was he standing under it?"

"Son, all that might as well have been in another language to me. Let me see if I got the gist of what you're sayin'. You're tellin' me that the guy you killed got crushed under somethin' as an accident?"

"Yes! I never meant to! If I could take it back, Uma, I would. I'd trade my life for his, I swear. He had a kid!"

"Oh boy." I blow out a mouthful of air while shakin' my head. "So… You didn't mean to kill him? You didn't have it out for the guy?"

Devin starts to sob uncontrollably. "God, no! How could you think that? You think I'm a murderer?"

"Well, yeah! You done told *Lawrence* you was gon' kill him just for not playin' your song!"

"I don't even remember that! I was blackout drunk! If I said that, I surely meant it metaphorically."

"You were requestin' songs about bein' some kinda psycho killer! *Qu'est-ce que c'est?*"

I can't help myself. I have to finish the line. *Great. Now David Byrne's voice is gon' be stuck in my head all doggone day…*

And it's not like I can do some karaoke and get it out!

I relax my grip a little on my glass and take another sip of my drink, not quite ready to let my guard down fully. But this klutz *is* clumsy enough to possibly get a man killed on the job. I feel like I might believe him.

"You did time for murder. I saw people talkin' about it on the internet."

"I got *manslaughter*, Uma. There's a huge difference. It means I had no intent—"

"*Chile*, I know what manslaughter means! I was married to a cop for many years."

"I got out on good behavior after two years. You don't get two years for murder. I was working a lift. I had just gotten my certifications. There's a basket that a light operator can stand in. We took it off to rig some lights, and I guess I didn't put it back on right. My friend was standing under it when I started moving the machine over to the side of the sound stage for the night and the whole basket came off in mid-air. I didn't have any *beef* with the guy. I liked him. He took a chance on me. He was the man who got me my start in the film industry!"

Makes sense. The kid's been self-medicatin' with alcohol since I met him. He seems like an idiot and a hothead but maybe not a malicious one, if I'm bein' honest.

"Where were you at one o'clock the day Lawrence was killed?"

Devin thinks for a minute. "I was in the infirmary. I hurt myself during limbo."

"Show me your injury."

"What?"

"You know. Your cuts or bruises."

"Can't. I just pulled a muscle. I bent under the stick and fell weird on my arm. Thought I tore my rotator cuff, but turns out I just strained it a little. They gave me some ibuprofen and sent me on my way."

I don't know if I believe him. The Funtivities Director said limbo started at one o'clock. I doubt anyone could have caused that much self-destruction in just a few minutes, even someone as klutzy as Devin.

My eyes settle on the bag he's been carryin' around all secretive-like. It is limply hangin' off the corner of his chair. My tone comes out like a blatant accusation. "Mind if I look in that sack of evidence you were takin' out to the middle of nowhere to bury?"

He makes a gross spit bubble when he opens his lips because he's been cryin' so hard. "Evidence? You think I'm going out there to hide evidence? You have got to be kidding me!"

"Fork it over, then." I hold out my free hand for it.

He glares at me for a minute with a look of anger, like he wants to knock me out but can't because I'm just some little old broad.

"You wanna stick your nose into everything, fine. Take it." He yanks the plastic bag off the chair corner and shoves it at me. It weighs more than I imagined.

I unfurl the man's shirt in it, a flannel one that I don't remember Devin wearin' the morning of the murder at breakfast. But, then again, he might have changed clothes.

I pull out the flannel, and all that is left is a gallon Ziploc of fine rocks and sand.

"Souvenir from Mexico?" I ask as I hoist it up with my age-spotted hand.

He nods at the bag. "You're holding my father."

"What?" I drop the bag onto the bar top as if the longer I hold it, the better my chances of possibly bein' possessed by the man's ghost are.

"My father died last month. They cremated him. In his will, he asked me to spread his ashes on the beach in Mexico. We spread mom's a few years back, somewhere around here. I rented a scooter to find a nicer spot to dump the ashes than at a port that reeks of cilantro." Devin lowers his head and mumbles to himself, "He hated cilantro."

"And the shirt?"

"It was *his*. I wrapped the bag in it because I'm a clumsy oaf and I didn't wanna puncture the Ziploc and find out I left my dad scattered all over the road."

All that is left in the bag is somethin' that takes my breath away.

A brand new selfie stick, still in the packaging!

A carbon fiber one.

Just like the murder weapon. No doubt, to replace the one he broke off in Lawrence's chest.

"What do you have *this* for?" I swallow hard, tryin' not to sound like I'm onto him.

"It's for taking pictures of yourself a little further away than your arm can reach."

"I know *what* it's used for, you dodo bird! I meant, what do *you* need one for?"

"I saw they had some at the photo kiosk. Figured I could get one and film myself dumping dad's ashes for my brothers. The nurse at the infirmary told me I should get one so I don't have to strain my shoulder taking vacation pictures. It's not like I have anyone to take them *for* me." He looks sad, like he's pitying himself.

I finish my drink and sit in silence for a minute takin' everything in. Finally, I slide the ashes, selfie stick, and shirt toward Devin and look into his eyes again.

"What can I do to convince you that I didn't kill that guy?" His dark eyes are almost piercin'.

I still don't know if I believe this kid. Especially, his alibi.

"There you are. I have been looking for you all day. *¿Cómo estás, mi amor?*" I feel a hand slide onto my back and the presence of a gargantuan figure next to me.

I follow Devin's gaze up to the tall, bald man by my side. It's Rinalto. He is flashin' a brilliant-white Cheshire Cat smile down at me like somethin' out of a fairy tale.

The creepy Grimm's kind. Not the charmin' Hans Christian Anderson kind.

Devin pulls some bills outta his wallet and tosses them under his empty bottle for the bartender. He scoops his things into one arm and looks up at Rinalto.

"Help yourself to my seat. I have to go handle some things with the scooter rental company." Then, Devin glares at me, hurt in his eyes. As he scurries off, Rinalto eagerly takes his place in the chair across from me.

"Listen, *Rico Suave*—"

Before I can finish, Rinalto grabs my hand and pulls it toward him, placin' a soft kiss on the back of it. "What do you want to drink? Anything. It is on me."

I'm torn between my desire to flee while screamin' *stranger danger* at the top of my lungs like Dolly would and the opportunity to catch even more of a well-earned buzz on someone else's dime.

I look at the bartender and mouth, *Same thing. One More. His tab.*

She nods.

"The usual," he says to her. She responds the same to him and then walks off.

"What do you want with me, Rinalto?" I huff. Just because he's buyin' me a cocktail, it doesn't mean I gotta pretend to be nice to the guy. "Isn't the FBI on the case now?"

"*Si.* That is why I came over. I am no longer the lead investigator, and I can be myself around you."

"You weren't being yourself before?" I raise just one eyebrow.

He chuckles. "You are feisty. I like you. You have," he snaps his fingers a few times like the word he wants is just out of reach, "*bite.*"

"Oh, I do. I got a lotta bite."

The bartender puts a sweaty beer down in front of him as well as a frosted mug from the freezer. Then, she pops a shot of gold tequila in front of him, too. He pours his beer into his glass and gives me a wicked grin. "I like a woman who *bites*."

Oh boy.

"I'm old enough to be your *madre*, pal. I have underwear older'n you."

He leans in with his shot glass and speaks lowly. "You are the perfect age. I love a beautiful woman in the autumn of her life. You have seen the world and experienced many worldly things." He slams the shot, and his eyes widen. "*Eres una puma.*"

"Puma?" I'm confused.

"*Si.*" Then he claws his hand and swipes at me like a jaguar, complete with the hissing.

Then I realize what he's tryin' to say.

It's not *puma* at all. He means…

Cougar.

Oh, dear lord.

I look at the bartender. "*Señorita?* Hey, make that mojito extra strong, *por favor.*"

19

"My Lord, my stomach was touchin' my back," I say as I throw my rumpled cloth napkin on the table beside my plate of spent oyster shells.

"I can't believe you eat 'em raw like that. Not to mention that pound of horseradish and hot sauce you drowned those suckers in," Cosmo says with a chuckle.

I wag my finger. "Crystals. It's gotta be Crystals. Don't gimme none'a that Tobasco nonsense. If it ain't the good stuff, I'm out."

"You must have an iron stomach, Uma Mae. What's your final count?"

"Four dozen."

"Good Lord."

"What?! They're small! Those things are all shell!"

I look at his plate, at what *was* a dozen Oysters Rockefeller and is now just a pile of cheese-encrusted hollowed exteriors. I think he eats like a bird to maintain that delightfully muscular physique. Guy's gotta be two percent body fat, if that.

"You called it. That's for sure. This place is very good." He pats his abs. "I'm stuffed."

"What's on your agenda the rest of the night?" I ask.

"I don't know. I am torn between goin' to that mixer Isa's been houndin' me about and takin' in one of the stage shows."

"The mixer?" I sigh. "I forgot all about that. That's tonight?"

"Yeah." Cosmo nods and then looks down at the remains of the mollusk massacre in front of me.

"I don't think I can make small talk with a buncha strange weirdos for that long. 'Specially since none of 'em are gonna live anywhere near me even if we hit it off."

Cosmo's eyes lift from my plate of meltin' ice and shells and settle on mine for a long time. He looks at me like he has a lot he wants to say, but doesn't know where to start. A warm smile spreads across his defined jaw.

I'm frozen, curious as to what he's thinkin'. My stomach flutters.

And I don't think it's from all the raw seafood either…

His mouth opens, and my name comes out of it, gentle and sweet. "Uma—"

Before he can utter another word, I see his eyes drift up to a spot several feet above my head.

"Uh, can I help you?" Cosmo asks.

All of a sudden, I hear Rinalto's thick accent. "There you are. I have been looking for you, Ms. Blanchard."

"Why?" I roll my eyes, still not turnin' around to look at him. "The FBI just as clueless as you are when it comes to solvin' an investigation? You need me to give another statement or somethin'?"

Cosmo dabs his face with his napkin and rises from his seat. "I best git before all this food hits me like a rock. I'll let you two discuss. Sounds important." He nods at Rinalto. Then, at me. "Thank you for the lovely dinner and company, Uma Mae."

Always such a gentleman.

They don't make 'em like Cosmo anymore, I'll tell you that much.

Without another word, his leather jacket is back over his tight T-shirt, and he is headed out the glass door back toward the concierge desk, and my romantic night feels thwarted.

"Rinalto, anyone ever tell you you're like a five-gallon bucket of ice water on any doggone situation?"

Rinalto flashes that alarmingly wide smile. "I am afraid I do not understand this American phrase."

I don't feel like explainin' what a buzzkill is in simpler terms, so I simply just slouch back in my chair.

"What do you need from me? Does the FBI need another statement?"

"*Dios mio*, no," he chuckles and sets down a glittery black gift bag next to my plate of spent shells. "They are examining everything the men and I put together right now. I am sure they will have a lead soon."

I can't stop starin' at the gift bag. "Rinalto, what is that?"

"I believe where you are from, they call this a *lagniappe*."

"How do you know where I'm from, *Cher*?"

Rinalto cocks his bald head to the side as if to say, *Come on, how stupid do you think I am?*

"Ms. Blanchard, I have sailed aboard cruise ships for almost fifteen years, and for the majority of those, my main port has been New Orleans. I recognize a sexy Cajun accent when I hear it."

"You meet people all over the world and you somehow think the *Cajun* accent is *sexy*?" I bark out a laugh. "Boy, you're crazier'n I thought! Heck, half the Lose-yanna natives I know sound like they all just had a stroke and can't do nothin' but lazily burble out mumbled responses when you ask 'em somethin'."

"Well, I think you sound," he leans closer, his knee touching mine, "like an angel."

Oh, dear lord...

I swallow hard and nod my head at the gift bag. "What's in there?"

He grins and shoves it toward me. "A gift. For you. I hope you don't think it is too forward."

"Frankly, Rinalto, I think everything you've done since I met you is forward, but I'm willin' to chalk it up to cultural differences."

"Open it." He lets the comment roll off him like water off a duck's back.

Hesitantly, I reach inside the bag, movin' the tissue paper aside. I feel a thousand scratchy, uniform nubs on somethin' cylindrical. I yank the item out. I'm floored the second I see it.

A rhinestone-encrusted snorkel.

"There is a matching mask in there, too."

"Rinalto!"

"You like it?"

"Why did you buy this?"

"I was watching you on the cameras, and I saw this capture your heart."

"Oh, Rinalto," I don't know how to break it to him that I thought this thing was doggone ridiculous, "I don't know what to say."

"Say you will go dancing with me tonight at the discotheque. I love to dance."

"Oh, no, there is no way I can accept this." I shove it back in the bag and push it toward him.

"Yes, you can. I insist."

"And *I* insist that you return it. Get ya money back."

He continues to smile. I can't tell if he's unfazed or if his face is simply stuck that way like an Alice in Wonderland character. "They do not allow returns for items that go in your mouth, *mi amor*."

"Well, then, *you* keep it. You'll look absolutely fetching in pink with your tan."

He howls with laughter, and a few people listenin' to the live pianist on the other side of the oyster bar whip their heads in our direction and glare.

Rinalto stands, walks beside me, and looks down at my ear, speaking low, tryin' to be sexy. "Are you free? I would love to give you a tour of the ship's bridge. The view from the wheelhouse *es muy pasmoso* at this time of night."

I rise from my chair, not botherin' to look at him. "Son, not only am I not *free*, but I promise you could not afford me." I glance up at him, annoyed. "Plus, it's a little obnoxious that you're usin' the ship's cameras to spy on me and track me down. Not only do you have a regular job to do, but you got a *murder* to solve on top of it. And it doesn't seem like you've made much headway in that department."

I press the gift bag against his hulking chest, and he looks down at me, a little wounded. "You wanna give me a gift? Solve the murder and reopen my doggone karaoke. All I wanted this whole time was to get drunk and sing my little heart out. I don't think I'm askin' for the moon!"

He takes a step back, leavin' me with the bag in my hand. The smile returns to his face. "Keep it. When you use it, think of me."

"Yeah, when I'm underwater, in the clutches of death's watery hands, starin' a doggone barracuda straight in the face, I'll be sure to think'a you." I roll my eyes.

"You sure you do not want to dance with me tonight?" He starts to cha-cha in place, and he suddenly reminds me of Gomez Addams, if he'd somehow been gene-spliced with 'Stone Cold' Steve Austin.

"I heard they just repainted the fin thing on the top of the boat, so I think I'm gon' be busy watchin' that dry."

"The funnel? No. They did not paint it." He looks dead serious.

"It was a joke. I'm… nevermind."

He just stares at me.

"Come on. I will beg if I must." He leans in, smiling that off-putting smile of his.

Rats. He ain't takin' the hint. Maybe I need to try a different tactic.

I force myself to burp. It smells like horseradish and raw mollusks. I act like it happens all the time, and I wave my hand, pretendin' I don't know I'm waftin' it right at him. "Ew, excuse me. Oysters really get my gut goin'. Half the time they go straight through me."

"No worries." His smile never falters, and I start to wonder if the guy is actually part robot.

"Do you salsa?"

"Oh yeah, I eat all kinds. Make my own, too, with tomatoes right out of the garden." I know he means the dance, but I'm playin' like I'm a dummy.

"No, I mean like salsa." He dances in place, shimmying his hips.

"Salsa? No. I guess I'm more into the flamingo."

"You mean the Flamenco?"

"I do a lot of tap," I say, ignorin' his question.

"Tap dancing?" He looks a little disgusted. A moment later, that bizarre smile returns. "I can teach you. I would *love* to teach you. For many years, I was an instructor."

He wraps an arm around my waist and pulls me to him so hard that it almost knocks the wind outta me.

Both ends.

"I could teach you the Rumba. It is the dance of love."

"I'm good." I grimace.

"Please. You are, how they say," he whispers into my ear, "*exactly my type*."

I shove away from him, annoyed. "Well, you are, how they say, creepin' me out. The answer is *no*, Rinalto. Go do a lap. It's a cruise ship. I'm sure if you looked around, you could find yourself thirty blue-haired floozies, at least one of whom might actually be down to clown with a young buck like you." I poke myself in the chest. "But this old gal ain't interested."

I pull away and head to the exit. At the door, I turn and holler over the music, "Rinalto, there's a cold-blooded killer loose on this very boat."

My words make the people at the tables around us perk up, eyebrows scrunchin', jaws slack.

"I suggest you spend less time chasin' skirt and do your doggone job. Catch him!"

20

The long walk around the Lido Deck did me a world of good. That is, until two mojitos in, when I looked over and saw Cosmo and some long-haired hussy chattin' like old friends at the singles mixer down the way. She was makin' him laugh. That really burned my roux to see. *I'm* the one who should be makin' that gruff-and-gorgeous man laugh! Not some aging Brooke Shields wannabe.

I imagine Harry lookin' down at me. Him seein' me salivatin' over some other man -- *no matter how handsome Cosmo Goodman may objectively be* -- woulda made him howl like a bayou *loup ga roux* when he done saw it.

Harry always *was* the jealous type.

Lord rest his sweet soul.

Finally, I get back to my stateroom, walkin' this length of long hallway with hideous carpet that looks kinda like the same one in *The Shining*. This whole windowless Octopus Deck does have that eerie Overlook Hotel kinda vibe to it, now that I think about it.

I scan my card and open my door to see the bed made, crisp, bleached sheets atop it. A crab made out of a terry cloth towel sits in the center of the comforter, and I snicker at the sight of it. I lob my gift bag of bedazzled beach accessories into my open suitcase on the floor, one I didn't bother unpacking.

What's the point? The cruise is only a couple of days. Working out of it's much easier.

Draggin' my tired self to bed, I swipe the fabric crustacean off hard. It hits the wall and falls into a rumpled pile in the chair beneath a mounted canvas print of a family swimming with a buncha dolphins in teal waters.

I kick off my shoes and face-plant on the bed. After a moment of layin' face-down in the sterile-smellin' sheets, I think about the flighty young man who does all the maid service stuff for my stateroom.

What was his name again?

I roll onto my back and hear two of my vertebrae pop, followed by a strangely satisfyin' sense of relief. Remind me to tip my complementary Oshannic chiropractor…

Really, though. What was his name?

Droopy. Apple Pie. *Drew Pye. That's it.* He's the one datin' that photographer that Lawrence had his eye on.

I picture them at the *Take That!* kiosk, her with a boba drink in her hand, indifferent to the shifty boy who just brought it to her. I remember the way he looked at her. It was a look that didn't exactly scream love. Or even lust.

It screamed somethin' like *suspicion.*

Distrust.

I don't know why I'm thinkin' of him all of the sudden. Maybe it's the fresh sheets or the fadin' scent of his body odor and sweat in this tiny room.

I picture him catchin' Lawrence starin' at his girl. Then, I picture him takin' one of the selfie sticks from his girlfriend's kiosk, unpackaging it, and then joustin' Lawrence right in the chest with it in the Hammerhead Lounge. Strangely, I can see it in my mind's eye, and I feel like maybe I've been leavin' a big-ol' honkin' thread of this investigation just danglin'.

That is the last thought I seem to have before I career headfirst into a deep slumber leavin' all the tungsten track lights in the ceiling of my stateroom still blastin' full force.

21

This mornin' hit me like a Mack truck. I'm feelin' the effects of having a body that is more mojito than water at this point, and I desperately crave one of those pickleball Bloody Marys I was talkin' to Cocktail about.

I soak my dentures and brush 'em, still in that haze between sleep and consciousness, like I'm in autopilot. I wrestle on a magenta tank top and white capris and slip on my sandals.

I grab my lanyards and glance into the gift bag at the ridiculous mask and snorkel Rinalto gave me. I chuckle and shake my head. Why these sorts of things even exist is beyond me. How I now own my very own pair of Liberace-esque swim goggles is more bafflin' still.

I shuffle out the door and down to the elevator. I stare at the buttons on the side. My finger is poised to hit the top floor where the bar near the pickleball court is, but my eyes settle on the label for the floor just above this one with the word CONCIERGE next to it.

Hmm. Today we'll be docked in the Yucatan. My family and I haven't done much together on this vacation, thus far. I've spent most of my time playin' Sherlock Holmes with a smart-mouthed eleven-year-old and runnin' from the Mexican version of Pepé Le Pew in dress whites. Might be fun to see what they have available for excursions at the port. Maybe doin' something together'll be a start toward makin' things right with Cosmo after that hulking numbskull ran him off last night.

A last-second audible has me jabbin' that button instead.

Another short hallway spits me out near the teal-blue and white three-story atrium, the cavernous mall-like piazza at the center of the ship. It is a perfect place for people-watchin' and formal pictures. A chandelier hangs at the top, but instead of the typical kind of crystals one might see, this aquatic-themed one has thousands of oval-shaped horizontal ones on long chains. If you squint your eyes, it looks like a school of glitterin' minnows swimmin' together in various directions, changin' course every time the ship sways. The ceiling is painted to look like ripplin' waves. Four ornate, spiral staircases swirling through each floor in all four corners are sculpted to look like octopus tentacles that all lead to one bulbous head in the middle. Beneath the head is a single grand staircase, designed as a ritzy place to snap photos or skip the molasses-slow glass elevator on the opposite side.

I see Duncan chasing Stokely around in huge circles with a fork on the level above through the thick glass railing as they both shriek. An adult is chasin' them, growlin', "Stop! Please, stop doing that!"

I breeze through the atrium, takin' the painstaking and somewhat gaudy oceanic details in.

At the concierge desk, I smile at one of the ladies behind the counter who greets me with an all-too-bubbly personality for this early in the mornin'.

"How can I help you?" she asks.

I fold my arms across the top of the concierge desk, which is some kind of acrylic masterpiece with a brown, sand-like substance on the inner ring and crashin' cerulean waves on the outer ring. It's custom and seein' it almost washed my brain clean of what I even came to talk about.

"Uh," I glance back up at her, suddenly remembering. In this moment, I'm grateful for all the Sudoku and crossword puzzles I do on the commode at home. I think they keep my mind sharp.

"I'd like to book a shore activity in the Yucatan, please, *Cher*."

"Of course! We have lots of Progreso shore excursions."

"What have you got? What's good?"

She gets very excited that I asked her opinion, and she gives me a response so enthusiastic that it feels like she gets a kickback if I end up bookin' it. "I always recommend the Chichen Itza Ruins package. With this one, you get to explore Mayan culture and see an absolutely captivating wonder of the world." She puts her hands up. "Now, that said, it is a *lot* of stairs and walking."

An image flashes in my mind of the sun settin' behind the gorgeous Mayan pyramid, me with a drink in my hand enjoyin' the peace and serenity of such a wondrous sight.

Then, intruding into the fantasy are my grandsons at the top of the pyramid, Duncan screamin' his head off because Stokely is tryin' to sacrifice him to the Gods for a good crop yield.

"No," I say firmly, shakin' the image from my mind. "What else have you got?"

"There's a cantina crawl. It's this huge party bus that takes you to the various bars and clubs all around Progreso. A member of our Oshannic staff keeps your glass more than half full the entire time, or you get your money back."

"As much as I would love to explore Mexico three sheets to the wind, I wouldn't be able to bring my grand-spawn on an outing like that. I'm tryin' to just meet my minimum quota of spendin' time with everyone so they don't whine that I ignored 'em all and actually enjoyed my vacation."

"I get it."

"What else ya got?"

"Let's see." She clicks on her keyboard for a moment and then smiles at me. "There is the pink flamingo expedition and beach adventure."

I recall the time I caught Duncan on the roof of my house huckin' rocks at a live pelican, and I shake my head. I don't trust that kid around a bird unless it's cooked rotisserie style and on his dinner plate.

"No. The boys aren't good with live animals. You got anything else?"

"Boys, you say? There *is* an ATV adventure."

"Dear God, no! Someone would end up in a Mexican hospital twenty minutes in with those demons."

Although the sight of Cosmo doin' wild tricks on a dusty trail on one of those things would *be quite a sight…*

She scrolls her mouse some more and finally gasps. "I think I've got just the thing. No live animals. No dangerous equipment. The kids would love it."

"I'm all ears." I snicker. "Seriously, *Cher*, I got to cover them a bit with my hair. When my kids were growin' up, they used to call me Dumbo."

She forces a smile and ignores the self-depricatin' joke. "This excursion also comes with a meal where the locals make these incredible tacos." She groans a little like she's enjoyin' the memory of ones she had in the past.

"You had me at tacos. What's the excursion?"

"The *Cenote Santa Rosa.* In this excursion, you all get to swim around in these *beautiful* underground caves. Oh, it's so neat."

"What's a *cenote*?"

"It's a water-filled, natural cavern. When limestone beds collapse, sometimes they open up to these beautiful watery underground cave systems."

"So, it's basically a sinkhole filled with rain?"

"I suppose that's one way to put it."

"We got a lotta those in southern Lose-yanna," I say with a laugh. "Is it pretty?"

"Oh my, it is one of the most beautiful things I have ever seen!"

"Sounds alright. Sounds like somethin' everyone can enjoy."

"After the tour-guide-led snorkel and swim adventure, afterward, up on land, the locals will serve you a traditional Yucatan meal with real *horchata* and these shredded chicken tacos that are just…" Her eyes roll in the back of her head for a moment, and I almost wanna give the girl some privacy.

I think of the bedazzled snorkel Rinalto gifted me, and it all feels like some weird kismet. *Not to mention, any excuse to spend time with Cosmo without a shirt on is a win in my book.*

Plus, real Mexican tacos? Sign me up.

"Yeah, you know… the kids would probably like to swim. We'll do that one."

"Fantastic. This package is on sale, too."

"Oh, girl, keep talkin'. You sound like an angel when you say stuff like that."

She giggles. "Everything's included. Even travel. A bus will take you out to the *cenote* from the port once we dock. Right now, with the sale, it's only $89 per person. How many in your party?"

"Let's see. Me, Cosmo, Daniel, Jane, and Isa. So five adults and then the two kids."

"Fantastic."

"Can you bill it to my room card?"

"Absolutely! No problem at all." She starts clickin' away at her keyboard. "For the walk to the *cenote*, we require everyone in your party to wear close-toed shoes. And before you can swim, you will be required to shower off any sunscreen or lotions, so you might pack some in a bag with some beach towels in case you want to reapply them afterward."

"Sounds good to me." I slide the lanyard with the card across the hyper-realistic surf frozen in time beneath the thick layers of clear acrylic, and she starts clackin' away to make the reservation. Finally, she hands it back, along with a few tri-fold pamphlets about the excursion.

"You are all set! When we dock at Progreso, just look for Cooper Nagilnick, your Funtivities Director. He is the guide scheduled for this one today."

"Yeah, I know the fella. His rusty curls and lack of butt should be easy to spot in the crowd."

"Enjoy the excursion, and thank you for sailing with Oshannic!"

22

With one of Cocktail's delicious spicy Bloody Marys in hand, I cruise down the Promenade level breezeway past the Poseidon Theater until I spot the Koi Casino's glowin' signage. It's sandwiched between two eateries with pun-filled names: *Just For the Halibut*, a seafood restaurant with upscale decor and a lit-up aquarium wall you can see from the breezeway, and *The Mullet Over Diner*, a greasy spoon fish-and-chips joint that wishes it were *Long John Silvers*.

I don't know how many more nautical puns I can take. Oshannic went a little overboard on the theme.

I see Cosmo and Isa inside and wave. I walk in and sit down at the small bar in the chair next to Cosmo.

"How'd you find us?" Cosmo chuckles.

"Well, it wasn't hard. When I didn't see you at breakfast, I figured you might be down here. Seems like y'all have been on a winnin' streak lately."

"You always had a keen eye for detail, Uma Mae," Cosmo says with a smile. I can't tell if he's bein' sarcastic or serious.

"I got you both a little somethin'. A little gift to say thank you for comin' on the cruise. I'm sorry I haven't spent a whole lotta time with y'all. I've been a bit preoccupied."

Cosmo shakes his head and deals himself a hand of Five Card Stud on the video poker machine in front of him. He takes a swig of his drink, somethin' clear with bubbly seltzer because he's always watchin' his weight, even on vacation. "Where there is a mystery to solve, Uma Mae is on the case."

"You say that like it's a bad thing," I elbow him playfully.

He shrugs and deals another hand. "It's not a bad thing. I just think it is a little strange that last time this kinda thing happened, all you could think about was goin' on vacation. Now, you're on vacation, and all you can think about is finding your perp again."

"You aren't the least bit worried knowin' there is a murderer walkin' around among us?"

Casual as ever, he says, "Until this very moment, I had not given it a single thought. But now that I am, no, I don't suppose I'm worried about it."

"Why not?!"

"Because there are over five thousand people on this floating shopping mall, Uma Mae. The likelihood that the killer is going to strike again is low. The likelihood that he would target one of *us* is exponentially lower. Heck, I go into the French Quarter twice a month to get a muffuletta from Mr. Ed's on Iberville. I've got a better chance of something happening to me while I'm in that area than I am on this boat. There are cameras all over the darned place. Heck, they probably already even got the guy. You just haven't heard about it because they aren't tryin' to draw attention to it."

I shove the card on my lanyard into the video poker machine and deal myself a hand of Deuces Wild. "That guy who so rudely interrupted our dinner last night is one of the head investigators. He said it ain't been solved yet."

"Oh." Cosmo seems like he wants to change the subject.

We play in silence for a moment, playin' our respective games.

"How was the singles mixer last night?" I finally ask, tryin' not to peel my eyes away from the terrible hand the computer just dealt me. I'm five deals in, and I haven't seen a single deuce yet.

"Oh, it was lovely," Cosmo says with a delighted smile.

I imagine he's thinkin' about that Brooke Shields-lookin' floozy I saw comin' onto him. My middle finger smashes the DEAL button a little too hard. "Well, that's good. I'm glad to hear it."

I try to contain my irritation.

Three, seven, nine, Jack, king.

Trash hand.

I take a long draw from my straw and choke. *Good lord almighty, Cocktail makes a spicy Bloody Mary!* I annihilate the skewered green olives and gobble down the pickled green beans as I fume.

I hear the sound like a record scratchin' and Isa punches the air joyfully on the other side of Cosmo. "Yes! I am on fire today, *Cher*!"

"*Mon Dieu*, girl. Dinner is on you tonight!" Cosmo jokes.

"Actually," I interject, slidin' two pamphlets over to Cosmo and Isa, "dinner is on *me* tonight. I bought us all a Progreso excursion."

Cosmo looks stunned. He studies the aquamarine water of the underground *cenote* framed by long strings of tropical sage-green foliage depicted on the cover of the brochure.

"C'mon, Cosmo. Swim in the gorgeous waters of *Cenote Santa Rosa*. Then, feast on local-made authentic Mexican tacos and fresh *horchata* with me, would ya?" I bat my lashes at Cosmo, my head restin' on the flattened backs of my hands like Shirley Temple.

Isa is the first to talk, her voice high and squeaky, "Oh my God, Uma! You shouldn't have! Thank you so much!"

Cosmo looks at me, his smile so soft and warm it makes me want to purr. We've never gone out on a real date, but with as handsome as he looks right now, if he suddenly asked me to marry him in this moment, I'd *heavily* consider it.

"Thank you, Uma Mae," he says. "That's very kind of you to do."

I deal myself another hand. It's crappy, and I'm already over this lame excuse for a casino. I'm spoiled by Harrah's in the quarter and L'Auberge in Baton Rouge. This rinky-dink little hole in the wall joint is as terrible as the ones outside of the strip clubs in Saint Amant, the sad ones that all the refinery workers blow their paychecks at.

I cash out. "I have to go give Daniel and Jane the info, but I will catch you both a little later? We can all go together. There's a bus or a shuttle or whatever at the port that'll take us there."

"You got it, Uma Mae. We'll be there with bells on," Cosmo says, his blue eyes makin' my feet feel like they're super-glued to the floor.

"Good. Maybe wear some shorts, *too*, though, Cosmo. There'll be children present." I wink, and Cosmo waves me away like the joke was a burp that came outta my mouth or somethin'.

As I head toward the breezeway to take my left toward the elevators, I see Drew Pye, the weird little shrew of a man who cleans my stateroom. He rushes right past me, never lookin' up, his ridiculous braided rat tail swayin' as he shakes his head in anger. He is cursin' at the floor, his fists balled up, growlin' like he's in the middle of an argument with someone.

Instead of takin' my left, my feet are on autopilot, forcin' me to go right and follow the angry weirdo from a safe distance. I hug the wall, ready to duck in somewhere the second he turns around, but he never does. He continues to the end of the breezeway, slammin' his hands on the stairwell door. It flies open, and I see him scuttle down the steps.

I check my watch. I got a little time before I gotta round up my son and his *Krewe du Crazy*.

You know what? I'm followin' him. *YOLO*, as my grandson always says.

As Drew scurries down the stairs, I trail behind as quietly as I possibly can. I'm already out of breath by the time I see the sign for Octopus Deck two, just one floor down. Drew keeps goin', his feet whiskin' him down the steps with youthful ease to the first floor.

I do my best not to grunt or groan at the toll the second concrete stairwell takes on my rickety old knees. I hear him jam the card on his lanyard into some kind of reader on the wall. It emits a long beep, then the door opens. I watch from the top platform of the final staircase as he slams the door wide and rushes through. I hurry down to reach it before it closes. The hydraulic hiss of the door closer stops abruptly when I slide my hand in the gap to disrupt the latch. I curse silently as my palm crunches between two pieces of rigid, unforgivin' metal.

Nothing is probably broken, but *dagnabbit*, that hurt!

I open the door slowly to see a long, bland hallway with drab, blue carpeting. The lights are white and make the gray walls look like some kind of sickly old hospital. Every room looks the same, just like upstairs, except here there are no frills, no decorative anglerfish sconces, no Overlook Hotel pattern on the floor. Just a blue carpet and hundreds of identical lookin' doors with tiny silver numbered placards.

Where did Drew go?

I don't see him down the hall, and none of the rooms have doors that are closin'.

"I'd ask if you're lost, but I know you aren't," a voice says behind my ear, scaring the ever-lovin' daylights outta me! I shriek and jump in place, whippin' my head to see Drew Pye standin' behind the door I'm half-through.

Once I realize I'm not gon' have a heart attack from fright, I straighten my posture and narrow my eyes. "No, son. I am not."

"You were following me down here, weren't you?"

I nod. "Yep. Sure was."

"You aren't supposed to be down here. This area is crew only."

"Yeah, yeah. I saw you in the hall cussin' to yourself, and I had a few questions I wanted to ask you."

"Questions?" He cocks one brow. "Questions about what?"

"About one dead karaoke host I saw ogglin' your girl the night before he died."

He thinks for a second and then straightens *his* posture, too. "Alright. Ask me, then."

"Did you kill Lawrence?"

He laughs. "Wow, you're just coming right out of the gate with a murder accusation?"

"Son, I'm about to be seventy years old. When you get to my age, you stop screwin' around with time-suckin' niceties and beatin' around the bush just because society wants you to. You stop datin' and go straight to marryin'. You beeline for that dessert bar at the buffet. And, above all, you *get* to the *point*. My time, what little might be left on this spinnin' blue ball in outer space, is precious, ya see?"

"You want to know if I killed Lawrence?"

"I didn't stutter." I step closer, serious and disgruntled.

He snickers again. "No, ma'am. I didn't kill Lawrence."

"Son, this ain't no laughin' matter. A young man -- albeit an *annoyin'* one -- is worm chow now, and someone on this very boat sent him to meet his maker long before his natural time. I happen to think that someone is *you*."

"This is ridiculous. Why would I ever do such a thing, ma'am?"

"Stop callin' me ma'am, kid. I hate that!"

He puts his hands up in surrender. I can tell he still ain't takin' me seriously.

"You saw Lawrence droolin' all over your girlfriend from afar, and you got jealous."

"Jealous of *Lawrence*?" He looks at me like my face is covered in writhing grub worms. "That's rich."

"Well," I look him up and down, "neither *one of you* is good lookin' enough for a pretty little gal like Jenny. I knew Lawrence for all of five minutes, and I could tell he was a pain in the behind, but you are no prize either. Maybe if you shaved off that ugly little rat tail and did somethin' with that hair."

"Did you follow me into restricted crew barracks just to insult my appearance? Or did you have some kind of proof, like *anything at all*, that would make me a suspect?"

I step back. Maybe I shouldn't be insultin' a potential murderer in a private area where I'm not even supposed to be.

"You had access to the murder weapon." I remember him eyein' the package of the selfie stick in my hand when I was at his girlfriend's photography kiosk.

"I don't even know what the murder weapon *is*, ma—" He stops himself before he says the rest of the word 'ma'am'.

I stare at him really hard. I can't tell if he's lyin' to me.

"You mean to tell me that on a boat this size, with all of y'all havin' these little close-knit relationships, that there hasn't been any chatter about the murder weapon? I don't believe that for a second."

"I work on a cruise ship. There are probably close to a thousand crew members aboard the Aspire, and you think we are all best friends?"

"Oh come on! Don't play me for a fool. I watched every season of *Below Deck*, and half the spin-off shows, okay?"

"I don't know half of the people that work on this boat!" He is gettin' loud now, frantically tryin' to make me understand. "You can't watch a TV show about super yachts and think you know how a cruise ship operates! You're insane."

"I'll have you know my last psychiatric evaluation came back just fine, and they let me go free."

"Wait, why did you get a psych eval?" He looks at me now like he's a little afraid of *me*.

"Doesn't matter. You're missin' the point. I don't buy for a second that you didn't know that Lawrence had been run through with the exact same doggone thing your girlfriend sells right there at her little kiosk!"

He looks horrified at this exclamation and covers his mouth with a tremblin' hand. Either he was some sort of theater nerd who could act with the best of 'em, or he really didn't know the young man had been stabbed. Judgin' by his introverted demeanor, I can't imagine the boy as some kinda thespian.

"Do you think it... Do you think it could have been Jenny?" he whispers, his eyes filled with terror.

I shake my head. "No. She's been cleared. Iron-clad alibi."

He breathes a sigh of relief. Then, he looks at me with sincerity. "Look, I couldn't stand Lawrence. The weirdo was always staring at Jenny. He annoyed everyone. He thought he was God's gift to sound design, which was admittedly obnoxious. He pretty much had no friends on the boat. But, I would never have done anything to him because of the hierarchy."

"Whaddaya mean, the hierarchy?"

"I know this may come as a surprise to you," he says sarcastically, "but I am not much of a 'people person.' If something happened to Lawrence, like it inevitably did, I would be next in line to move up from housekeeping into his position. They act like it's a promotion, but I'm awkward. I'm not extroverted. I have Asperger's. Having to interface with a bunch of drunks fighting to sing out of key is my literal, waking nightmare."

"Then, just tell your boss you don't want the promotion."

"It doesn't work like that on the Aspire! You go where they *tell you* to go when you've got no stripes, like me. And you say 'thank you,' and you do the job." He looks like he's gon' cry. "When they reopen the Hammerhead Lounge," he swallows hard, "I'll have to host all of the events there."

He starts breathin' like he might hyperventilate. He shoves his head into the corner of the hallway like a three-year-old that's been put in a time-out.

"Alright, relax. Calm down. Don't go passin' out on me, kid."

"What… Was… He… Stabbed with?" Drew asks between big choking breaths.

"Excuse me?"

"You said… It was something… At Jenny's kiosk?"

I think I believe this introverted little weirdo. It doesn't feel like an act to me. It feels like he's just deeply awkward.

After a moment, I decide to confide this particular detail of the investigation to him. "A selfie stick. Carbon fiber. Same kind she sells right there in her little photo shop."

His head pops up like one of those red things in a turkey to let you know the bird is done. "My buddy, Marvin, just bought one of those yesterday. I saw it because… Jenny's been acting kinda cold to me lately, so I've been trying to be nicer to her."

"Why's she icin' you out? You two have a fight?"

"No," he says, depressed. He can't make eye contact with me. "Something is going on with her lately. Something's up."

"She tell you what's wrong?"

"No. And I've asked. Repeatedly." He sighs heavily. "So, lately, I've been trying to put in the extra effort, you know? I've been leaving her little gifts and buying her that boba stuff she likes."

"It's very good, by the way. Suckin' up chewy wads of tapioca in a drink sounded disgusting, in theory, but I must say I'm leavin' this cruise a convert. I take back every mean word I ever said about the stuff."

"Yeahhhhh, that's great." He looks annoyed by my interjection. "Anyway, I was on my break, and I brought her another drink. Marvin was there at her kiosk."

"Interestin'."

He narrows his eyes. "No, not really. We hang together out all the time. He's kinda taken me under his wing since we both started here. Sometimes we time our breaks so they all sync up, and we meet at Jenny's kiosk since it's convenient for them. Yesterday, Marvin... He bought a selfie stick from her shop. Said he broke his and needed another."

His mouth goes wide, and his hand rises to cover it. He looks like he just found out he's been adopted his whole doggone life.

"Well, there you have it, son. He bought it to replace the one he used as a murder weapon." I don't say it like a question. To me, it isn't. The pieces are startin' to come together. "You said your friend is named Marvin?"

He nods.

My eyes bulge. "His last name wouldn't happen to be Button, would it?"

He looks at me, confused. His hands slowly drop back down, and he looks dazed. "Yeah, it is. But most people call him Cocktail, like the movie, because he's always flinging bottles in the air."

"Well, kiss my *etoufee*." I shake my head.

"He works at the—"

"Oh, I'm well aware. He tends at the swim-up bar near Jenny's photo kiosk. He's the best bartender on this swayin' vessel, *Cher*." I look around the drab hallway for a second. "He does take a lot of pictures of himself. Surely seems like the kinda guy who would have one of those things."

"On this boat, they make us post pictures to social media. For most of us, it's annoying. But for guys like Marvin, selfies are more of a sport."

"What do you mean, guys like Marvin?"

"I mean, you know, *good lookin' guys*. Marvin won the genetic lottery. He gets told he looks like Tom Cruise, like, five times a day."

"Does Marvin have a temper?"

"No! That's the thing. He's so laid back that it's frigging annoying sometimes. Nothing ever seems to ruffle his feathers. He bunked with Lawrence all that time, and he hardly ever said a bad word about the guy."

"Wait, so he was Lawrence's *roommate* here on the ship?"

"Yeah, he said Lawrence was weird, but that the guy mostly just sat in bed and worked on music on his laptop with his headphones on when they were in the room. Marvin said they never had anything to talk about, so they were just like ships passing in the night most of the time. Heck, I heard Lawrence complain about Marvin *exponentially* more than Marvin ever complained about him.”

“And why is that?”

“Well, because Marvin gets around. You know, when you look like he does, there’s no shortage of women who wanna rock the boat with you.”

“Great,” I growl, “now I’m gonna have that catchy Hues Corporation song stuck in my head all day.”

“Marvin’s a bit of a player, so I’m sure Lawrence had to endure a bit of a parade of women through his cabin throughout the months. But he never really had beef with Lawrence. Or anybody, really.”

“Any idea how he would have possibly broken his selfie stick if he didn’t skewer Lawrence like a campfire marshmallow with it?”

Drew shakes his head.

“Hmmm.” I glance down at the key cards hanging from an Aspire-themed crew lanyard around Drew’s neck. “You’re a maid, right?”

“Housekeeper. But… Yes.”

“You got somethin’ on that lanyard akin to a skeleton key for this-here boat?”

Drew straightens and stares at me. “Why?”

"Well, I was thinkin' if you could let me into Lawrence's room, maybe I could find a clue or somethin'."

Drew laughs. "You're kidding, right?"

"Do I look like I'm kiddin'?" I glare at him. "Do you think I'm in a position to waste my own precious time with jokes like that? I'm supposed to be on a bus to some *cenote* soon, and I haven't even told half my party that we're goin'!"

"Why on earth would I risk my job for you?"

"You wouldn't be riskin' it for *me*. Heck, you could watch me the whole doggone time and make sure I don't steal or muss nothin'. You'd be riskin' your job for your best friend. If this investigation led little ol' me to think he might be a killer, you had better bet the FBI is gonna make those same connections once they get their butts in gear. But if we could find a clue that leads us to the killer, or even somethin' that totally exonerates Marvin, like his old broken selfie stick, well, you'd be a real hero, son. Plus, Lawrence's cell phone wasn't by his body, you know. Maybe he left it in his room that day. Maybe it's got a clue or somethin' on it."

"That is all *such* a long shot. You know what's *not* a long shot? Me getting caught with a guest on the crew-only level of the ship, breaking into my friend's room, and rustling through a murdered man's things!"

"We can crack this case, Rat Tail! I know we can. You just gotta let me in there."

"No way."

"Hey." I stare at him. "Imagine for a moment how your girlfriend'll treat you if you were the *hero* who brought a cold-blooded killer to justice? She wouldn't be snubbin' you then. Heck, I'll bet once word got out about your bravery, Marvin's bed wouldn't be the *only* one shimmyin' at night."

It is the best case I can make to manipulate this doughy dingus into lettin' me in that room.

He studies me for a long time as if he's debatin' it all in his head.

Suddenly, the hallway door behind me swings open, and my blood turns arctic. Drew cups my mouth with a hand that smells like a blend of lemon furniture polish, rubber, and talcum powder, and two men in dress whites breeze past us. If they'd have looked back even once, they'd have seen us plain as day.

Finally, Drew looks at his watch and then whispers angrily to me. "You have four minutes in there, and then you're gone. And if anyone asks, I will deny this until my dying day."

23

Day 4 - *11:37 pm*
Marvin & Lawrence's Crew Stateroom
Squid Deck 1

The second Drew opens the door for me, I gasp at the size of the crew room. I feel like I've had shoe boxes bigger than this place.

"*Two* people inhabit this space?" My jaw might as well be on the floor. This place is the size of my closet in Killjoy. There are two bunk beds built into the wall that seem barely long enough for an adult male of average size to lie flat on. On the wall by the bottom of the bunks, there's a small wardrobe built into the wall that is just pitifully small. To my left is a bathroom only large enough for a commode, a tiny sink, and a teeny shower. The four-foot strip of blue, carpeted floor space is littered with Aspire uniforms, flip-flops, dress shoes, and colorful men's briefs. I grimace at the sight of it all.

"This is inhumane. They got y'all crammed in here like anchovies in one'a them tins."

"It's literally just barely enough room to sleep and shower," Drew murmurs, lookin' around nervously. "But, get inside! We need to get out of this hallway right now."

"Cool your jets," I say as I tiptoe in through the mess on the floor. Drew follows me in and closes the door. He glances at his watch. "Three minutes and thirty seconds."

"You're like NASA gettin' ready for a launch. Just gimme a one-minute warnin' and zip your mouth the rest of the time so I can concentrate."

Drew steps into the bathroom, pretends he's closin' his mouth with an imaginary zipper, and takes a seat on the commode. It's pretty much the only place he can exist in here while I poke around.

"Alright. Cell phone, broken selfie stick, written confession… Any of these things'll do." I say it more as a joke, but stressed out Drew ain't laughin'.

I rifle through pants pockets, searchin' for anything I can find. I lift the covers on the bottom bed. Still nothin'. I search the closet, if you can even call it that. In one pair of pants rumpled on the closet floor, I find a couple of wadded pieces of white paper, which I snag. I look at a laptop and a set of big, honkin' canister headphones. I can tell they're Lawrence's because they bear a sticker of another Anime woman with a massive back-strainin' bosom. I open it up and hit the power button. As soon as it springs to life, it asks me for a passcode. I huff and shut it quickly. I don't have time to be tryin' random combinations right now.

I look for books or some form of entertainment, but all I find are a bunch of gaming magazines.

I groan as I climb the ladder toward the top bed, but it's clean, as if someone turned the place down after Lawrence died, and it ain't been touched since.

Out of places to look, I unfurl the wadded paper in my hands. It looks like a few receipts. I study them.

One for a bottle of aerosol sunscreen from some place called *Beach Vibes*, dated Friday. Charged to a credit card.

One for a seven-dollar container of hair gel, dated Thursday, charged to a credit card.

One for a hundred-and-forty-seven-dollars worth of alcoholic beverages at a bar in the Nawlins port, dated Thursday. *Good Lord, that's a lot of Irish Car Bombs!*

Aha!

There is one for a selfie stick at the *Take That!* kiosk, dated yesterday! Charged to crew account: MBUTTON.

This confirms what Drew said in the hallway.

I unfurl another receipt.

Drew grumbles. "Ew." I glance over to see him pinchin' the very edge of a pair of lacy women's panties. He holds them up makin' a disgusting face. Then, he spins them around like he's investigating them.

"*Don't be a pervert*," I warn quietly.

"These... Look..."

He doesn't finish the sentence because I cut him off, holding the last receipt in the air. "Looks like you and Jenny aren't the only ones who like boba. Ol' Marvin here has a sweet tooth, too!" I hold up a receipt for *The Boba Factory*. "Purchased two boba teas. One chai. One Taro milk tea. Both charged to crew account MBUTTON."

Drew looks at me in horror and then looks back at the panties. He can barely get the words out. "Oh my God, I… I *recognize* these."

I scoff. "Yeah. Sure you do, kid."

Suddenly, my eyes bulge in their sockets. Not from some sort of mental revelation, though. It's because of the two voices panting at the door's exterior. I panic and look around for a place to hide in this oversized coffin-of-a-room. I try to shove in the bathroom, but Drew pushes me away.

"There's no room! Closet!" His whisper comes out as a growl over the beep of the key card.

I hear a woman giggle as I cram myself into the closet and try to close the door from the inside. It won't stay shut, so I hold it with my hand as two bodies burst in from the hallway, writhin' in passion, fused together at the mouth. Marvin's hands are tangled in long, messy lengths of black hair as he backs her against the wooden base of the top bunk.

All of a sudden, the lyrics to "Rock the Boat" pop back in my head like some kinda brain worm, and I find myself mouthin' the lyrics of the chorus as I watch the amorous couple. I start to wonder how I'm gonna make my getaway, or if I'm just gonna have to witness the whole dirty deed. Marvin's a young man, so I'm hopin' it's brief.

His mouth moves down the woman's neck and then to her chest. I fight the urge to gasp audibly as I see that the woman is none other than *Jenny Applebaum!*

Marvin and Jenny mumble somethin' to each other, a frantic back and forth followed by dual giggles. Through my gap in the closet, I see the bathroom's pocket door glide open, Drew Pye now on his feet and furious.

Jenny's head lolls over as Marvin unbuttons her pants, and she screams bloody murder, juddering against Cocktail's chest, scramblin' to re-button her uniform blouse.

"Are you *kidding* me?" Drew asks both of them, unsure who he is more hurt by: his girl or his *supposed* best friend.

"What the…?" Marvin bellows, clutchin' his chest. "Drew?! What are you doing in my stateroom?!"

Jenny scurries behind Marvin like she's usin' him as a human shield in the heat of battle.

"She said it could've been you, and I didn't believe her," Drew says, his eyes locked on his double-crossing bestie. "I didn't think you were capable!"

"Who? What? I am *so* confused." Marvin takes a step toward him, and Drew snarls like my Chihuahua, Cocodrie.

"The old bat said you probably killed him. I thought it couldn't be you, not in a million years. But now, I think maybe you killed him. Out of jealousy, maybe. You saw him looking at Jenny, and you snapped."

"Who?" Marvin shouts. "Are you talking about Lawrence? You think I killed *Lawrence*?"

"What old lady?" Jenny finally asks.

I take that as my cue.

Showtime!

I fling open the door and walk out, shakin' my splayed palms like one of Bob Fosse's backup jazz dancers. "This old lady, actually."

Jenny hears the voice comin' from behind her. She screams and does a one-eighty. Marvin panics, backin' up against the bed.

"How are you all in my room?! What is a guest doing on the crew deck?! Both of you… Get out!" Marvin points to the door.

Drew wads the pair of black panties up and hurls them at Jenny. "You dropped these."

Jenny unfurls the lacy bundle. A look of pure embarrassment spreads over her flushed face. She stuffs them into the pocket of her uniform pants and stares down at the short carpet, mortified.

"Where's Lawrence's cell phone?" I just come right out with it, jammin' my fists on my hips.

"How should I know?!" Marvin's voice goes high. He's angry as all get-out. "I wasn't his keeper!"

"What is happening right now?" Jenny seems dazed.

Marvin clutches her protectively to his chest and shouts. "Get. Out. Of. My. Room!"

"Where's the selfie stick?" I yell right into his handsome face.

"*Excuse* me?" Marvin looks appalled that I have the gall to ask him anything.

I hold up one of the receipts. "You bought a new one yesterday. What happened to the old one?"

"I lost it." He bobbles his head. "Actually, I think someone might have taken it."

"Mmmm. Likely story. How convenient that you would lose it right around the same time it ends up speared into the chest cavity of your bunkmate."

"What? You mean Lawrence was…?"

"I know the hot ones are sometimes airheads, but you're not foolin' me. You're not *that* dumb."

"I thought someone strangled him! That's what I was told."

"Sure," I say sarcastically. I'm not buyin' it.

"I wasn't anywhere near that lounge at the time of the murder, Uma. I already got cleared by the investigators."

"And what *miraculous* piece of evidence did you have that cleared you?"

"They just looked at the metadata on the photo I posted from the Bloody Mary bar. The one by the pickleball courts."

"What the heck is metadata?"

"Seriously?" Marvin is heated.

Jenny steps forward to try to lower the temperature of the situation with a soothin' voice. "Every time you take a picture of something with a smartphone, it saves all of the information about that photo. Like, where you took it, what aperture you took it at, what size it is, and, also, *when* you took it."

"Why show them this supposed metadata? Why not just send them to the cruise social media where y'all are postin' this stuff?"

"Because you can *schedule* those posts," Marvin growls. "I can set a different time for those to post if I want. The metadata is unchangeable. It's imprinted in the photo's information, like device DNA. The investigator knew there was no way I could have taken a photo of myself and a guest with her loaded Bloody Mary and make it to the lounge in time to do a dang thing to Lawrence Fordham."

"Wait, you can schedule your posts?" I feel like I have brain freeze from suckin' down a boba smoothie too fast.

"Yeah, people on this ship do it all the time. Some people like to take all their photos for the day all at once and schedule them for uploads at different intervals so they don't have to take pictures all day. I, personally, *like* taking selfies and stuff, but some people really hate it."

"I see."

"But the metadata is unchangeable, so they cleared me first thing."

"So… I guess the only thing you're guilty of is bein' a lousy friend and a scoundrel then."

Marvin lowers his head, humiliated. "I'm sorry, Drew."

"Don't talk to me, Marvin. You're as dead to me as Lawrence is."

With that, Drew storms out of the room.

I take the opportunity to creep toward the door, as if I could somehow make it out of this tiny cube unnoticed.

"Well, then… Thank you for your time. Sorry to have bothered you."

I step out into the hall and peek my head through the door one last time. "Oh, and Jenny, you called it with the boba. Seriously good stuff."

24

"I had a feeling I might find you in here," Dolly says as she waltzes in through the front elephant door of the lounge and sees me sittin' in one of the cushioned booths in front of the stage.

"I was just walkin' past on my way to go find my son, and someone said that they opened the lounge back up to the public about an hour ago," I say glumly, staring at names I've scribbled onto one of my excursion pamphlets across a photo of the emerald waters of *Cenote Santa Rosa*.

Dolly slides in next to me, *uninvited, I might add,* and peers down at the names. "Those your suspects?"

I nod, tossing down the pen I found on the floor near the spot where we discovered Lawrence's corpse. The stage reeks of bleach.

Dolly picks up the writing utensil and spins the pamphlet toward her. "Who's Cocktail?"

"Marvin Button. One of the bartenders."

"He's scratched through."

"Yeah, because he ain't a suspect now. He had an alibi. Showed me some metadata thingy on a photo he took around the time of the murder up by the pickleball courts."

"You scratched off Jenny, too."

"She had a photo. One from her digital camera. That weirdo, Rinalto, cleared her pretty much right away."

"Drew Pye? Who is he?"

"He was my maid and also Jenny's boyfriend up until a couple of minutes ago when we broke into Marvin's room and caught him tryin' to fornicate with Ms. Applebaum. He's been cleared, too."

Dolly grimaces. "Yikes. Drama."

"You can say that again."

"Why'd you cross off Devin? He said he was going to kill the guy at karaoke. Everyone heard him."

"He was at the nurse's station at the time. Said he hurt himself playin' limbo, even though that timeline doesn't seem right. Limbo wasn't til noon, so he'd have had to have hurt himself right off the bat."

"Why'd you cross him off, then?"

"He's too stupid to have done this and also avoid detection. He'd have tripped on his way out the door and stamped Lawrence's blood right on the floor out there." I point out the door at the hallway where a blinding spot of sun is bouncin' in off the gleaming tiles. "Plus, I rented a scooter yesterday, and I followed him into the middle of nowhere. Thought he was dumpin' evidence. Turns out it was just his poor daddy's ashes."

"But… He murdered someone already," Dolly says.

"Manslaughter. I looked up some news articles about it online yesterday to confirm his story. The moron got someone killed on set, did his time, and got out."

Dolly sits in silence for a moment, using the bleach-scented pen to doodle the outline of a fish by Cooper's name. "Why haven't you crossed off the Funtivities Director yet? Didn't you say he had an alibi?"

"He did. He posted pictures from limbo at the time of the murder."

"Dang." Dolly starts to cross his name off the pamphlet, but I stop her.

"No. Don't."

"Why?"

"Marvin mentioned it's common practice on this boat to sometimes stockpile a buncha social media pictures for one's quota and schedule them to upload throughout the day automatically. Cooper showed me his alibi photos on social media. I have no clue if he posted those right then or if he scheduled them."

"But wasn't he hosting limbo at that time?"

"Well, Devin claimed limbo was earlier. So I don't really know what to believe."

"And you have Rinalto on here as a suspect. How come?"

I wave her away. "Oh, that's just because he's a creep. He's been followin' me around the doggone boat, and I just wouldn't put nothin' past him."

Dolly flips over the pamphlet and traces the edges of the *cenote* longingly. "Can I see your phone?" she asks, her tiny hand splayed, ready to grab.

I stare at her for a long time. Then, I finally say, "It's in my room. Why?"

"I was going to look on the cruise app and see what time it said limbo started on there." She shrugs. "Nevermind."

"I gotta go round up my son and his family and get ready for the shore excursion anyway. Come with me. We'll go grab it."

I grunt like a rutting buck when I get out of the seat, and we start toward the door.

Suddenly, Dolly perks up, her face confused. "Wait, do you hear that?"

"Nope. I don't hear diddley-squat, kid."

She takes on the characteristics of a German Pointer and walks toward the edge of the stage where we found Lawrence's body.

With reluctance, I follow her.

Two steps in, I hear it, too.

A ringtone.

An 80s song.

Tommy Tutone.

As we get closer to the hosting stand and amplifier stack, I realize *exactly* what it is. *It is the faint jingle of Lawrence's missin' cell phone!*

"It's somewhere over here!" Dolly drops to her knees with a thud so hard it makes my entire body cringe.

The instrumental chorus trills one final time, and then the room falls silent again. Dolly and I search the area frantically, our one chance to find the device while it's ringing now gone. Dolly clambers across the floor and flattens her face against the laminate. I wince, thinkin' about the pool of blood that was right there only days before.

"I see something!" she yells, staring into the gap beneath the amp stack. "It could be the phone! It's hard to tell from here. It's pretty far back in this slot. Maybe two feet or so."

Suddenly, I remember the fallen pens tryin' to roll under there when I was talkin' to Lawrence about singin'. Now, I picture the annoying host in the final scuffle of his life, fightin' with his murderer. I picture the person assaultin' him, the phone with the well-endowed Anime cartoon flyin' outta Lawrence's hand, the boat rocking, and the device slippin' right into the gap beneath the amplifiers.

"That's got to be it, Dolly! I just know it! That was his ringtone!" I look around. "Maybe we could get something to fish it out, like a wire hanger."

"Mommy Dearest, we're in a karaoke lounge. Where are we getting a wire hanger?"

"How do you know who *Mommy Dearest* is?"

"I told you, I can watch whatever I want! Duh."

I shake off the rude reply and look around. "What about my pamphlets? You think you could slide it toward you with those?"

"I don't think they're gonna be strong enough with this big gel case. It kinda feels wedged. I think we need to lift these big black things up to get it."

"They're amplifiers, kid." I eye them for a moment. "Say, if I hoisted them up a touch, do you think you could reach it?"

Dolly sits up and glares at me. "If your frail arms can't hold them and you end up dropping those on me, they're gonna crush my arm."

"Fracture. *Maybe*. Crush is a little extreme."

"So lemme get this straight. You want to lift that stack of speakers up with your feeble, wimpy little old woman arms and put some stranger's kid in harm's way so you can get a dead guy's phone?"

I stare at her for a moment and finally say, "I'll buy you a boba if you do it."

Dolly sighs and flattens onto her belly on the floor. "Fine. Let's get this over with."

I scurry over to the amp stack and try to figure out the best angle to lift or tip it to give her access.

"But I'm getting a large. You're not getting cheap on me with some kid's size, you hear me? I want the biggest one they got."

"Stop your yammerin' and get ready. I don't think I can hold this thing up more'n a couple of seconds."

"Ready when you are."

I count us down from three and groan as I lift the corner of the stack of amplifiers. The whole pile nearly topples backward, and I have to correct quickly to keep the thing from flipping. I don't know how much these things cost, but I sure as heck don't wanna be responsible for replacin' them!

Dolly grunts as she dislodges the phone. My grip slips. Before I can even think to warn the kid, her hand -- and the phone -- make it out from underneath just in the nick of time.

SLAM!

The amplifier stack smacks down hard and Dolly glowers at me, absolutely fuming. "Thanks for the heads up that it was coming down! You almost just crushed my arm!"

"Hey, kid. It slipped. Stop whinin'. You didn't get hurt."

Dolly lobs the phone at me, and I barely catch it. A busted piece of the selfie stick's clamp is still fused to the rubbery gel cover.

"Well, I'll be!" I pluck the piece of the clamp off the case and shake it at Dolly. "I've been lookin' for someone replacin' their selfie stick this whole time. Turns out Lawrence mighta been stabbed to death with his own!"

"We should check his phone for clues. See who he was texting. See if he had any recent issues with anybody," Dolly says as she snatches the phone right out of my hand.

"Hey. Rude!"

Dolly ignores me and walks off with it, examining the screen. There is a huge spiderweb of cracks and glass dust, presumably from the impact during the fatal assault.

"Geez. I can hardly see anything with all this damage." She scrubs the screen against her lavender shirt with puff-painted lettering that says 'Drama Queen.'

"No!" I screech, swipin' the phone back the second I realize what she's doin'. "Now ya done wiped off any fingerprints that might've been on it!"

Dolly looks at me with eyes like the Coyote that awful moment before gravity sets in when he realizes Roadrunner has tricked him into runnin' off a steep cliff.

"Oops!" she says, after a long pause.

I pace with the phone in my hand, the one that surely only contains the fingerprints of an old woman and an eleven-year-old child now. "What do we do? I probably should give this thing to Rinalto to hand over to the FBI, but I feel like I really need to see what's on it!"

"Hey, those guys had their chance to search the crime scene for clues already. You snooze, you lose. I say we get in there and poke around a little. If we can't find anything, we can always turn it in then."

"They got us on camera, kid! Our story will be as flimsy as a Nawlins levee if we turn it in later and they check these tapes."

Dolly shrugs. "I'm willin' to take that chance."

"You're a minor. If you obstruct justice, worse thing that's gonna happen to you is you get *grounded*. Which, knowin' how feral your mama lets you be, even *that's* a stretch. Me on the other hand, I'm old enough to know better. I could do real time."

"They're not going to lock up a hundred-year-old woman for not giving up a phone they missed, Uma."

"I'm sixty-nine!"

Dolly chuckles and tries to hide her smile. She forces herself to look serious. "I think you have a serious case of chicken-itis."

I narrow my eyes at the kid and sigh. "I guess it… Can't hurt to… You know… Jus' take a peek, I s'pose."

I press the buttons on the side of the phone, and the cracked screen lights up. The lock screen is askin' for a numerical passcode.

"Oh, kiss my grits!"

"What?"

I turn the lock screen to face her. "It wants a doggone number code!"

"Hmmm… try 1-2-3-4-5. He seemed dorky enough to have something idiotic like that."

"Don't be ridiculous. No one is gonna use that as their passcode," I say as I spin around and secretly try those exact numbers where Dolly can't see me.

DENIED.

Eh. Worth a shot.

I glance at the giant clock on the lock screen and realize the time. "Oh, no."

"What?" Dolly spins around with flair, hands on her hips, tennis shoes projecting lights like an LED dance rave on the laminate of the karaoke stage.

"The flippin' time, kid! I gotta round up the fam for this excursion I booked."

"Oh." Dolly sounds sad.

I don't really know why, but the tone of her voice makes me feel a touch of guilt.

"I think Daniel and Jane said they'd be eatin' lunch with the kids at *The Rusty Harpoon* up on the Gulf Deck. C'mon. I'll get you that boba."

Dolly manages a sad smile and nods.

25

With my sugary boba in hand, I lead the way to Daniel and Jane's table at the pizza parlor. It seems like a weird name for the place until I see a waitress walk past me with a sizzlin' breadcrumb covered seafood pizza. I can smell the peppers and garlic on it, and I make a detour to the front register with Dolly.

"Welcome to The Rusty Harpoon. What can I get you?" the young man at the register asks.

"Gimme a slice of that Clams Casino pizza." I point to one of the pie-shaped pieces underneath a dome light behind a piece of glass. "It smelled amazin' as that lady walked one past us."

"Sure thing. And you?" He looks at Dolly. Then, she looks at me again.

"Go on. I'm buyin'," I mutter begrudgingly.

She smiles. "Pepperoni, please."

He nods, charges my room card, and serves us up two heapin' slices of pizza on a checkered paper plate. We thank him and make our way through the maze of people to Daniel's table. He dabs his mouth with a paper napkin.

Still chewin', Daniel says, "There you are. We've been lookin' all over for you."

"And why's that?"

As I start to stuff my face with warm pizza, Jane interjects, so quiet I can barely hear her among all the chatter. "Daniel and I booked an excursion, and we were wondering if you'd watch the boys for a bit."

"It's funny you should say that. I already booked us for a group adventure. My treat." I reach into the pocket of my capris and toss the brochures on the table. The one with my list of suspects lands face up. Embarrassed, I remove that one from the pile. "We're goin' snorkelin' at the *cenotes* and then doin' a traditional Mexican dinner right there with the local folk. Ain't that somethin'?"

"Actually," Daniel speaks up. "Jane and I are going to tour the ruins of one of the old Mayan temples. It's considered one of the wonders of the world."

I chuckle to myself, recalling how I talked the lady at the concierge desk out of bookin' that one for us all. "And why didn't you wanna take the kids?"

Daniel tilts his head and widens his eyes. "I don't think it's wise to start teachin' these two about human S-A-C-R-I-F-I-C-E."

Dolly snickers and looks at Duncan, who is tryin' to grind his grease-covered plastic knife on the edge of the table into something that looks suspiciously like a prison shank.

"Wise choice," I mutter. "I already paid for your tickets, though."

"So did we. You weren't answerin' your phone, Ma. I tried to call." Daniel leans back in his seat. "So? Will you watch them?"

I look at my grand-spawn. "Y'all wanna go snorkel at a *cenote* and eat chicken tacos?"

Stokely stands up so fast his chair goes tumblin' to the floor in a loud clatter that turns heads. His arms outstretch like someone bein' struck by lightning. He shrieks with excitement.

"I'm gon' take that as a 'yes' I guess." I look at Dorothy. "You wanna take my son's ticket and help me wrangle these two chicken-heads?"

Dolly nods wildly, peelin' the last pepperoni off her slice of 'za and eatin' it with her fingers.

"Good. Maybe you can keep 'em from killin' each other, or at least some poor innocent bystander."

Dolly salutes me like a soldier with a hand mottled by cheese grease. "I'll do my best."

"Duncan, Stokely? You think y'all can be ready to roll out with me when this ship docks in half an hour?"

Duncan and Stokely don't answer. They just scream in unison.

Jane mouths the words '*Thank you*' to me silently, her hands pressed together like she's about to pray.

"You two enjoy the ruins. I'm gon' go hunt down Devin and see if he wants this last ticket. Better that than lettin' it go to waste, because I'm positive it ain't refundable."

26

The massive bus rattles down the dirt road. We are all packed in like sweaty sardines watchin' the small clay houses and rickety wood shacks pass by. Wild dogs run in the street, avoidin' cacti without a thought. Some of the homes don't have any windows at all. Just holes in the side like some giant, busted-up terracotta pot or somethin'. I see a woman pinnin' laundry to a clothesline. I see a man chewin' gum in his open doorway. A block over, I see kids hittin' a ball with a stick. We pass lush greenery, dusty trails, run-down gas stations, and tattered red, white, and green flags.

Devin is sittin' between Duncan and Stokely a few rows up. Stokely is wearin' the flaming-red *luchador* mask I gave him, and Duncan has gum stuck in his hair. They are tryin' to smack each other by reaching across Devin, shakin' him with every violent *whack*. He takes a generous chug from a metal flask with a touristy sticker of Cozumel adhered to the outside, a trinket he surely overpaid for from the market near the scooter rental facility yesterday.

Dolly keeps pressin' her mouth between the seats in front of Cosmo and I to talk to me. "You should try 5-4-3-2-1."

Cosmo looks at me. "What's she talkin' about, Uma Mae?"

"It's just a little game we're playin'," I lie. Then, I lean forward and get close to the fabric-padded gap and whisper, "*I already tried that one. Didn't work.*"

I lean back in my chair. Cosmo stares at me.

"What?" I shrug.

"You're still tryin' to play detective, aren't you?"

"Are you kiddin' me?" My shrill voice goes high, and I surely just gave myself away.

Cosmo's hand slides into mine, and he gives it a reassurin' squeeze. "Sweetheart, you shouldn't be gettin' mixed up in all of this. I'm beggin' you. Look around, Uma Mae. You're on *vacation*. It's the last full day of this-here cruise. I'm begging you to just… Try enjoying yourself, for once. Let all this To-Catch-a-Murderer nonsense go. Let the professionals handle this."

I nod, unsure what else to say. He squeezes my hand again and then brings it back to his lap where he re-opens the worn paperback of some presumably tense political thriller.

I stare out at all of the other people on the bus and take a deep cleansin' breath, one that smells faintly of sunscreen, cumin, dry dirt, and chipotle seasoning.

Three more quiet minutes later, I pull out my cell phone and open the Aspire app to poke around. In the search bar, I type in Lawrence's name. Nothin' comes up. I type in Cooper's and a photo of him lookin' friendly pops up with a short bio about him. Beneath it is a list of events he is scheduled to host. I look at the upcoming events. Let's see… the *cenote* excursion happening now, a black tie soiree at seven, the hairy chest competition tomorrow mornin' at ten, and another art auction right before disembarkation.

I scroll down further to a list of past events. I click the link for Lido Limbo. It takes me to a page that says, 'Oops! This event has been rescheduled for 11:00 a.m. with Marta Miller."

My eyes bolt open wide, and I audibly gasp.

This thing says Cooper didn't even host limbo!

And on top of that, it was rescheduled to an hour earlier!

That means… Devin could have been tellin' the truth about bein' in the nurse's station at the time of the murder!

I scroll down and click on the app's link to the Aspire social media page. It pulls up a cache of saturated photos that make Aspire look as wild as Burnin' Man.

There are photos of guests in feather boas and wicker hats, some with bikinis, some with water wings, some with white scarecrow noses gooped with sunblock. There are pictures of Marvin and guests hoistin' sweaty cocktail glasses in the air at the swim-up bar. There's a trove of culinary shots: gourmet burgers, shrimp cocktails, raw oysters on ice, lobster pizza, grilled tuna steaks on arugula, and piping-hot seafood bisque. There are snapshots of people cheerin' at the casino and dancers doing high-kicks wearing next to nothing on the Poseidon Theater stage. There are photos of veterans next to a giant American flag and a shabby-lookin' stand-up comic in flannel on a tiny brick-backed stage. There is a picture of Dolly with two hot dog buns crammed in her mouth at once like some sort of greedy squirrel tryin' to pack carbohydrates away for winter.

Then, there's a picture of Cooper Nagilnick, his hands holdin' one end of the limbo pole down by his thighs like some sort of heavy dumbbell as a young boy with wet hair bends down like a crab to clear it. People all around him are cheerin' in full party mode.

I click the photo, which takes me to a larger version of the same image with a comment section on the right. There are heart reacts and generic comments. There's a timestamp that says, 'Posted two days ago at 14:12 p.m. EST.'

That would've been 12:12 p.m. here. Pretty much the exact time that Lawrence was murdered.

I stare at the photo for a moment. I notice somethin' strange. Nagilnick's wrists are exposed in the picture, both side by side, the skin pale and bare. But Cooper has that lopsided, weird-lookin' little dragon tattooed on his wrist. I saw it at the Muster Station when he gave us the spiel about the lifeboats. So, unless he got it removed -- and then re-tattooed -- this *has* to be an old photo!

Suddenly, my beach bag starts to buzz by my leg, and I hear the all-too-familiar jingle of that famous Tommy Tutone song. My face blushes red with embarrassment as I kick the bag against the wall with my foot.

Dolly whips around in her seat and rises to her knees, her wide eyes peerin' down at me from over the cushioned headrest. "Answer it!"

Tense, I shake my head, a subtle movement to tell her silently to shut up.

Cosmo looks over, confused. "What's wrong, Uma Mae? Aren't you going to answer it?"

"No." I swallow hard. "Like you just said, I should relax and enjoy my vacation."

"Well, yeah, but a call like that, it could be important. What if it were one of your kids?"

I don't want to have to explain that it isn't my phone or why I am walkin' around with a crucial piece of obstructed evidence in a criminal investigation on a federal level, so I rummage through the rolled beach towels and bejeweled snorkel set and take Lawrence's phone out of the bag. I press it to my ear closest to the vehicle's window so Cosmo can't tell that it ain't mine.

I click the button to answer it, and a pre-recorded spam call chirps in my ear. I feel a bit of relief and take a deep breath.

"Well, hello, dear! I haven't heard from you in a dog's age," I say to the inhuman robo-caller on the other end. The pre-recorded message hangs up in my ear, and I say, "I'm so sorry, darlin'. This isn't a great time to talk. I'm on a vacation, you see. I'm down here in the Yucatan enjoyin' time with some great people…"

I wink at Cosmo, and he goes back to readin' with a soft smile on his face. Meanwhile, Dolly is gaping at me as she hugs the headrest like a stuffed animal.

"Yep. No problem, doll. I'll give you a call when I'm back in Killjoy, I promise."

I pretend to hang up, and I stare at the lit-up lock screen and the number buttons that beckon for a passcode. I don't blink until the screen goes black. I lay my head back against my headrest, my heart racing.

Out of nowhere, Isa starts to hum the Tommy Tutone song, bobbin' her head. "Such a catchy tune." She hums some more, and I hear her stumble through some of the numbers in the chorus, "8-6-7-5-3-hmm--mm-mmm-mm,"

As if a bolt of lightning had struck the bus on this sunny, cloudless day, Dolly and I perk up in unison, both puttin' everything together at the same time. She frantically points from Isa to Lawrence's phone. "Try it."

"It makes so much sense," I mutter.

Dolly smooshes her face into the headrest. "That was who he was gawking at the whole night."

"Jenny-Jenny. It's *got* to be. He was infatuated with Jenny Applebaum." I swallow hard, grateful that Cosmo is back to readin' his book. I shift in my seat, tryin' to obscure the phone with the beach bag on my lap. I click the button on the side of the phone to wake it up. On the numerical pad, I punch in the numbers from the chorus.

8675309.

A satisfying click sounds, and I'm suddenly on a new screen, his apps and camera roll now available for access. I wanna scream, but I can't. So I settle for flashin' the newly-accessed screen at Dolly and watching her pretend to faint in her chair.

27

"What's on the phone? Anything juicy?" Dolly whispers.

"I don't know yet. Cosmo was sittin' right next to me, and I didn't wanna have to explain anything I found to him. I don't think well on the spot like that."

Dolly nods and stares at Duncan and Stokely as they scheme quietly among themselves. She's right to be wary of those boys if she wants to come away from her vacation with all limbs intact and fully operational.

Clad in our swimwear and freshly-rinsed in the warm outdoor shower to get all of our lotions and sweat off, the whole gaggle of us head toward a pile of damp, neon orange life vests, each strappin' into one the right size. A local woman ensures that we are properly fitted and clasped in tight before motionin' for us to follow Cooper.

"Alright, everyone, follow me," Cooper Nagilnick says in his loud, outdoor voice. It bellows through the cavern as he enters.

As we walk in, I am absolutely floored by the sight of this place. I thought the outside was pretty, what with all the banana trees and lush greenery, but the inside is a sight I will never forget. This place is amazing. The pamphlets don't do it justice.

Single file, we all follow the butt-less Funtivities Director down a set of rickety wooden stairs that twist around, huggin' the rock wall. Every so often, the stairs turn, givin' the option to either continue goin' down or to veer off onto a stone outcropping to view the *cenote* from high above. The bottom of the stairs plunges right into the vibrant, turquoise waters.

Fifteen-foot-long dreadlocks of foliage are growin' down from a gaping rock opening in the ceiling above. A beam of heavenly light pours down through it, illuminatin' the bright blue water. This looks like a scene outta some James Cameron animated movie that cost a bazillion bucks to make. This *cenote* is part swimmin' hole, part cave, and one hundred percent fascinatin'.

"Look, Stokely! Birds! Quick, find some rocks!" Duncan exclaims. His life vest swishes as his arm swings up to point at the circlin' creatures flappin' above us. They seem to be huggin' the craggy ceiling in their circular flight.

"Okay!" Stokely starts lookin' around for weapons of assault when a Latina woman scrambles over and tries her best to be sweet.

"No, *niños*. Those are not birds. They're bats. Many bats call these *cenotes* their home."

Stokely looks at Duncan for a second, unsure what to make of this information. Finally, a wicked smile spreads across his lips as he points at Duncan. "I'm gonna get one to bite you and make you a Mexican vampire! You're gonna have to live on earth forever!"

The guide gives me a worrisome look and murmurs to me, "Please, don't let them throw rocks at the bats, ma'am."

"Yeah... I won't."

Cooper speaks to the gaggle of life-vest-clad vacationers. "Alright, Claudia here is going to be your tour guide and tell you all kinds of fun facts about the *cenote* as we swim through. So, everyone, please stow your personal items here at the entrance. Security will watch them until we return. We're going to do a full circle through the entire *cenote* as a group, and then you can either swim or tour the grounds for a bit until the *horchata* and taco luncheonette is ready. Okay?" He claps too enthusiastically.

Cooper receives a lackluster verbal confirmation that we, thirty-or-so people, heard him.

While Cooper and Claudia help everyone get off the bottom of the wet stairs and into the water, I slip Lawrence's cracked phone into my rolled-up towel in my beach bag. I casually stow the bag on one of the rock outcroppings near some of the other vacationers' stuff.

"Quick. Don't draw attention to it. People are looking," Dolly says with her teeth clenched as she adjusts her life vest. She's assigned herself to be my lookout, this eleven-year-old partner in *literal* crime.

"Quick, quick!" Cooper waggles his hand for us stragglers to join the others in the water. "We can't start the swim unless we are all together."

"Yeah. Sorry. Just grabbin' my snorkel and mask." Embarrassed, I pull out the bedazzled set that Rinalto bought me and laugh at how ridiculous it looks. Meanwhile, Cooper helps Dolly slip into the water.

"Ohhhhh! That's so warm!" She giggles. It's the first time she's sounded like an actual kid since the moment I met her. "I thought it was gonna be freezing, but it's so nice!"

"Last one in is a rotten egg fart," Duncan hollers, his voice scarin' some of the bats right out through the hole in the top of the *cenote*.

"That's you, Mee-Maw!" Stokely laughs like a chipmunk.

"That's not very nice," Cosmo tells them, his fit form bobbin' in and out of the blue-green waves as he wades. "And it's rotten *egg*, not rotten egg *fart*."

Both children giggle like the juvenile dinguses they are.

Cosmo smiles and waves to welcome me into the water. *"C'monwithit,"* he mumbles, a common Killjoy phrase that blends all the words together. It is usually the most impatient thing you'll ever hear a true laid-back Cajun say.

"Here we go, Ms. Uma," Cooper says as he lowers me into the tepid water, his arms extended as if I'm a basket he's sendin' down the river Jordan. I stare at the dragon tattoo on his wrist.

"That's a nice tat," I lie. "You ever regret it?"

Cooper smirks and looks at it. "Not really. I kinda regret not picking a different *artist*, but I don't regret getting it."

"I'm surprised they let you have ones that show in a hospitality job like this."

"Eh," he shrugs as he gets in. "I had the job a few months before I got it. No one seemed to notice after. Or if they did, they haven't said anything about it."

"Is it new? Looks new." Another lie. It looks well healed. I strap the pink rhinestoned goggles across my eyes and feel the pressure in my nose as the seal forms against my skin. The attached, blinged-out snorkel scratches against my cheek.

"No. It isn't. I got this for my birthday a couple of months ago. Celebrated turning twenty-eight on Bourbon Street. When we were docked at port, I slammed one of those big, green grenades and stumbled into the first parlor I could find."

So he's had it for months.

Funny... *It sure wasn't in his cruise pictures two days ago when Lawrence was murdered...*

I slip in and tread water, followin' the last of the buoyant crowd to a small tunnel in the cavern where the more eager half of the group has already followed Claudia through.

Several quiet minutes later, I'm once again astounded by the beauty of this place. I breathe through the snorkel and look at the lumpy, rod-like stalagmites and rock formations down below. The sight of teal waters fadin' into navy blue darkness beneath me is not somethin' I will soon forget. Overhead, mineral-rich stalactites hang like muddy icicles from the ceiling. Eventually, the rock walls narrow into a series of tight, low tunnels, which eventually spit us out into more expansive caverns.

I feel absolutely tiny in a place like this.

Cosmo and Isa get into a splash fight with my grand-spawn, and it makes me smile to see them all getting along so well. Dolly stays by my side, quietly doin' a backstroke, studyin' the rock formations above us. Every once in a while, she smiles over at me, content. I realize that with her mother constantly AWOL in her life, this is probably the most attention she's had in the last few *months*. Combined.

Forty-five minutes later, we all lazily return to the main cavern of the *cenote*.

"Check it out. Aren't they neat?" I point to the bats flutterin' around the beam of light with a finger wrinkled up like a raisin. Stokely lets out a war cry that sends 'em all dartin' right out the hole in the top again.

"Can we swim a little bit longer?" Duncan begs. "*Those* kids are!" He splashes water at five kids playing Marco-Polo.

"As long as you stay here where we can all see you, that's fine," I grumble. "I'm gettin' out, though. I'm gettin' all pruny."

"Me, too." Dolly gives me a glance that says she's up to somethin'. I know she's dyin' to snoop on Lawrence's phone with me.

Stokely swims toward the other kids and informs them he's playing, too. The other kids seem hesitant.

Dolly pulls herself out onto the tall set of stairs. She holds a hand out. I take it and groan as I make my way out of the water. Dolly looks up at me. "We gotta see what's on it."

"*I know. Patience, Grasshopper,*" I say as we dump our wet life vests in a woven basket.

Together, we casually head up the steps to the platform with my beach bag. I dry off a little with my circular towel. It features a cheeseburger on one side. I toss Dolly one that looks like a breakfast plate of bacon and sunny-side-up eggs. She wraps hers around her shoulders like a shawl. I wrap mine like a skirt, and we sit side-by-side on a little shoddy wooden bench overlookin' the water. I look around, unable to see where Cooper or Claudia ended up. I imagine they're probably somewhere outside coordinatin' the dinner.

"Here goes nothin'," I say as I type the numbers into the lock screen on Lawrence's cracked phone again. Dolly lays her face against my upper arm, tired from all the swimmin'. She seems anxious to see if we can find anything of value.

I poke around in some of the apps, accidentally clickin' things and gettin' flustered. "Ugh, I hate these new smartphones. I never know where anything is."

"Here. Allow me," Dolly says, holdin' her pruny little hand out.

I hand the device over to her. She sits up, and her fingers start to fly. First, she is in his email inbox, scrollin' through messages, siftin' through deleted items, and pokin' around in the junk mail.

"Wow, he was *not* very popular."

"Heck, I coulda told you that much, kid."

Next, she checks his messaging apps. *Nothing of use.*

Then, his social media accounts, of which there are only two. Neither seems to have anything but cruise photo uploads and a few heart reacts.

"Let's check his camera roll," she says excitedly.

"Dear God, hand that over to me. If you get scarred by a buncha nudes, I'll never be able to forgive myself."

Dolly relinquishes the phone to me, and I turn away from her, doin' a quick scroll through the roll to make sure she isn't about to get any sort of *adult* education. I really don't want to have to explain to her mother why her child is traumatized. Finally, I turn back and let her see the screen.

"Yeah, he didn't really seem like the type," Dolly says.

"I'm sure I don't even *wanna* know what you mean by that."

"Let's look at his most recent stuff first, anything that seems like it was from this cruise."

I nod and scroll to the photos toward the end of the roll. There are a few of the karaoke singers that I'm sure he took to fill his Aspire picture-posting quota. There is the girl who absolutely *butchered* a song by Journey, the scrawny teenage boy who sang a surprisingly good Kelly Clarkson cover, and the *fabulous*, burly man in his forties who performed Bette Midler's "The Wind Beneath My Wings" and dedicated it to his long-time partner. There was barely a dry eye in the room.

The final three pictures on the camera roll are just useless shots of Lawrence in his booth. Nothin' juicy to blab to the FBI about.

I spin the camera roll to a random set of much older photos. They look like they were taken back when Lawrence first started, before he began to wear on everyone's nerves. There are photos of the Aspire, his bunk, Marvin eatin' cereal in his underwear on the floor of their shared stateroom. There's a picture of Jenny, who isn't aware he's taking a photo. There are shots of him and other crew members out of uniform, drinkin' booze straight from the bottle in Cozumel. And there's a selfie of Lawrence and Cooper. Lawrence is clearly trashed. Cooper looks sober. He doesn't look as amused as Lawrence is.

There's another photo that catches my eye, a selfie of him and Cooper Nagilnick in padded chairs, gettin' tattooed with the same dragon tattoo. Cooper's is on his wrist. Lawrence's is on his upper arm. I go into the photo's metadata.

The photo is four months old.

Just like Cooper said.

It's proof that the limbo photo Cooper posted at the time of Lawrence's death was an old one.

"I feel like Nagilnick's been lyin' this whole time. He most certainly lied about his alibi. The Aspire app says limbo was moved up an hour and hosted by someone else entirely, which corroborates Devin's story and pokes a hole in Cooper's bigger'n that one in the ceiling over there."

I point to Devin, who is one outcropping down from us, sippin' from his flask, wet legs just danglin' limply off the edge of the rock over the water below.

"Curious," Dolly says with a nod, the Watson to my Holmes.

"The photos on the cruise's social media show Cooper put up some limbo photos around the time of the murder, but he doesn't have that tattoo in any of the photos he posted."

"You said they can take pictures in the morning and schedule posts throughout the day to meet their quota.

What if he did the same thing, but with an old unposted photo of him hosting limbo before he ever had the tattoo?"

"Yeah, that's *exactly* what I think happened. Cooper reeks of this murder, but I have no clue how to actually *prove* he did it."

I look back down at the camera. There is little else of value in the photo roll as far as I can see.

Flustered, I hand the phone to Dolly. "All that tryin' to figure out the doggone passcode for nothin'."

Dolly looks out at Cosmo, who peels Duncan off the back of some other kid and quietly reprimands him. Duncan was probably tryin' to drown the poor girl. Thank goodness everyone's wearin' a life vest down there.

"What do we actually know about Lawrence?" Dolly asks, more to the ether than to me.

"That the loser had no real friends other'n Cooper, who got him hired."

"And?"

"And... That he was just shy of full-blown stalkin' Jenny Applebaum, who was probably in his stateroom often havin' trysts with Marvin, which had to really eat Lawrence's craw."

"I don't know what a tryst or a craw is." Dolly moves on. "We also know he was a horrible karaoke host."

"True. We also know that he liked Anime characters with boobs too heavy to lift without havin' back problems the whole second half'a her life. And we know he was allegedly spendin' all his free time aspiring to make music for video games."

Dolly shifts on the bench to look at me again. "You're kidding."

"No, a couple of people said it, actually."

Dolly peers back down at the phone, and her fingers start flying, swiping through apps, clicking on search bars, and typing stuff in.

"Aha. There's a whole trove of music files on here. Maybe there's a clue in that."

I sigh and lean back against the rock wall. "Ugh. Give it up, kid. Face it. We got nothin'. Might be a wild goose chase. Cooper lyin' about hostin' limbo technically ain't a crime. For all we really know, it could have been any one of the sunburned fools on our ship. Heck, for all we know, it was just a random, senseless act of violence. He ticked off the wrong person, and they stabbed him with his own selfie stick. End of story."

A fantasy soundscape starts playin' from the phone. Cinematic synths echo a poignant series of notes, each held for a long time. I gotta admit, while I'm not into video games, it doesn't sound half bad.

Dolly abruptly clicks on a new track, a jauntier soundscape, somethin' that makes me think of someone in armor rompin' through a field of tall grass.

She plays another. There is a patter of rain overlaid on the dark track, one that feels suspenseful, like a detective trackin' a suspect in a noir movie.

She clicks on another, and it isn't music at all. It's talkin'. A woman and a man seem to be arguing.

"Oh my God. Stop starin' at me, you friggin' creep! How many times do I gotta say that before you get it through your thick skull?" The woman in the recording sounds an awful lot like Jenny with her thick New York accent.

The man mumbles a pathetic response, and she growls. I can hear her stomp away.

Dolly clicks another recording.

It's Lawrence. *"Voice note to self: Make an upbeat song for kid's game similar to the Spiro or Jumping Flash II soundtrack for portfolio."*

The next audio track is another attempt at a video game score, one that feels hyperactive and fast, like I imagine Stokely's mind after he's eaten an entire bag of the licorice sticks I hide in my sock drawer. One of the notes of the song screeches long and loud, bouncin' off the walls of the underground cave like we're a band blastin' music in some kind of concert venue.

Everyone looks at us.

Several people enjoyin' the serenity of the sacred nature-made landmark glare at us.

One lady drying off on the rock platform nearby growls, "Do you mind taking that outside?! That's really loud!"

I feel embarrassed. Dolly rises from the bench and tugs me by the arm, insistin' I stand, too.

"Come on, Uma. Let's go listen to the others outside, where we aren't gonna get dirty looks." Then, Dolly sticks her tongue out at the woman.

The woman looks at me. "You need to get control of your grandchild!"

I laugh at the absurdity. I can't get control over my real grand-spawn, much less someone else's child. But, instead of arguin' with her, I holler down at Cosmo. "We're gonna step outside and see the ruins. Meet us out there when you're done swimmin'!"

I see Cosmo raise an arm out of the water and give me a thumbs-up. Behind him, Isa is tryin' to quietly resolve some kind of dispute between the boys.

Dolly and I make our way up the stairs to the blindin' tropical oasis above us. Banana trees with tattered leaves loom overhead providin' the only shade anywhere around. In front of us lies the gorgeous outdoor portion of the *cenote*, a disc of rich blue amid all the tan rocks and tropical greenery.

Dolly and I make our way over to the hole in the earth that leads down to the portion of the cave where Cosmo and the kids are. I walk to the edge and peer down to the water, my legs feelin' like jelly at the incredible height. Knowin' these *cenotes* are just sinkholes makes me suddenly feel like the ground I'm standin' on is gon' break away, and the watery cavern beneath is gonna swallow me whole.

A bat shoots out at me, and I jump back. I shiver and walk over to Dolly, who is sittin' on the stone ruins of some sort of sacred Mayan altar with Lawrence's phone.

She ignores all of the beauty and history around her and stares down at the shattered screen of the device. "There's only one more audio file. It looks long."

"Crank the volume and push play," I say.

Dolly taps the screen. I take a seat on the rocks next to her, and we listen as we stare out at this glorious, sunny postcard-style snapshot of Mayan paradise.

The final track is more people speaking. Two men this time. One sounds like Lawrence.

"Hey."

"Hey. You here to reprimand me again?"

(Long pause)

"Look. She's too sensitive, okay? It ain't a crime to look in a girl's direction."

"Lawrence, it's not just her. You've been getting a lot of complaints lately. From the guests and the crew. Heck, even your own roommate—"

"Marvin's got a problem with me, too? Are you kidding me?! That guy has a new girl in my room every other night, always moaning and giggling. I can barely get any sleep!"

"It's not just Marvin. It's everyone. Why do you think you're stuck doing karaoke? Lawrence, it's because you have a friggin' problem with everyone! I stuck my neck out

*to get you hired here so you could get out of your mom's
stupid basement!"*

"Ugh! What do you want from me?!"

I pause the track abruptly and look at Dolly. "The
other voice is definitely Cooper. Nagilnick was the one
who got Lawrence hired on."

"Interesting." Dolly nods and presses play on the
audio file again.

"I want you gone!"

The way Cooper says the word 'gone' sends a chill
straight to my bones.

"You don't have the authority," Lawrence says with a
laugh. *"Now, if you'll excuse me, I have to meet my quota."*

Then, there is a slight clatter. Plastic jostling.

*"Put down the selfie stick. I'm talking to you, moron!
You have been an absolute thorn in my side since you got
on this boat."*

There is a pause between them. Then, Lawrence's
voice sounds frantic.

"Hey, get away from me! What are you doing?!"

*"You never should have come. I never should have
vouched for you! That was so stupid! Before you got here, I
loved my job! Now every day someone is complaining
about you or is angry at me for getting you hired! I should
have known better. You did this in school, too! I'm always
guilty by association with you. But your mom was always
begging me to include you. You make me miserable!"*

The voice I presume to be Cooper's roars, like he's lungin' at Lawrence.

"*Stop it!*" Lawrence sounds like he's choking.

There's a scuffle.

More movement.

"*Stay back!*"

"*I should have done this a long time ago!*"

More skitterin' around. It sounds like Lawrence swings his selfie stick like a bat, and it connects with meat. There is more indiscernible noise, and then another impact of some kind.

There's more clattering, a *thud*, then a loud *smack*.

Lawrence pleads for Cooper to stop.

Cooper growls.

Their voices sound far away, as if the phone has just slid to the place beneath the amplifiers where Dolly and I found it.

There is a *snap* and a final "*Noooooooooooo!*" from Lawrence before the sound of three sickening impacts.

Lawrence goes silent, save for a single wet gurgle and the tappin' of what I assume are bloody fingers on linoleum, like he's tryin' to find his phone to call for help.

A pair of feet races away and up carpeted stairs. I picture Cooper racin' to the back doors of the Hammerhead Lounge that lead to the kitchen, presumably because he knows there's no camera coverage there.

Dolly and I sit and let four minutes of near-silence play, the faint sounds of Jimmy Buffett's "Margaritaville" oozing out of the phone as we both gaze at the azure waters in front of us.

We finally found our answer.

Cooper Nagilnick.

The Funtivities Director, of all people. The man hired to make the cruise excitin'.

Well, I guess for Dolly and me, he oddly enough did just that. I'm excited, alright. I feel like I'm about to have a heart attack. My chest thumps.

Suddenly, we hear more faint voices comin' through the busted phone. I assumed the rest of the track would just be dead air, but, to my surprise, I recognize what sounds like my own voice.

"Lawrence?" A pause. *"Lawrence Fordham? You hidin' in here somewhere?"*

"Someone over there?" I hear Dolly ask on the audio file. Her words are followed by a long pause.

Then, a frantic, *"Kid, go fetch help!"*

"Is he..."

"Now!"

"Okay! Jeez!"

I look at Dolly, my eyes wide with horror. "Dorothy, we missed witnessin' a brutal murder by all of four minutes."

Dolly doesn't know what to say.

"You should have been there. Maybe you could have saved him," an all-too-familiar voice says behind me.

Cooper Nagilnick!

Before I can so much as gasp, I hear Dolly shriek and see a man's hand strike her hard, hittin' her like she's a full-grown man. Dolly falls to the rocky ground, strugglin' to right herself.

I feel an arm wrap around my throat. It squeezes like a snake, and I claw at the hideous dragon tattoo on his wrist to try to get it free enough to get some air. But that hand clamps on his other arm, and the squeeze increases.

I can't get out any noise.

I see stars. The edges of my vision start to blacken.

I can't breathe.

"Let her go!" I hear Dolly scream. Then, I see a barrage of fist-sized stones flyin' past me, glancin' off the busted walls of the sacred Mayan ruins, some smaller ones rainin' down into the foliage-draped hole of the cenote. I hear the faint hollerin' of the people below, Cosmo's angry voice yellin' for "Whoever is up there, stop it this instant! You're gonna hurt someone."

I know he means the rock rain. The moment feels ironic because someone is getting hurt up *here*, too. It feels like Cooper is crushing my windpipe!

I hear him growl in my ear. "You couldn't just leave it alone, could you? You had to poke around and dig up all this nonsense."

He kicks Lawrence's busted phone into the wide hole. It takes two long seconds to splash into the water of the *cenote*, our only tangible proof of Lawrence's killer submerged in a pool of rainwater and guano.

Dolly screams again and fires another barrage of rocks at our backs, one of them beanin' me right in the back of the ribcage.

It doesn't matter, though.

I'll be dead soon.

As Cooper starts to spin me around to face Dolly, I hear a man's voice now. "Oh, no you don't!"

I hear the sound of metal crackin' against Cooper's skull and see the glint of Devin's flask as it hurtles through the air. Cooper's grip relaxes, and I feel a half a second of relief before the horror sets in…

Cooper is fallin' down the hole.

And he's takin' me with him!

Paradise disappears, and I scream as I plummet into the giant sinkhole. I catch a glimpse of the water far, far below. It feels like it takes forever to reach it.

Two seconds is a mighty long time when you're falling to your death.

The moment I feel myself slam into my cold, watery grave, it is exactly as I always imagined death would be.

A light switch flipped.

Everything fades to black.

28

"Oh, my God!" I hear a woman cry.

Isa.

What the heck is she doin' in heaven?

"Is she going to be okay?" This time, a man's voice. "I didn't think…"

There's sobbin'. I feel a kiss on my lips, warm and watery. Air forces its way into me, breathin' life into my dead spirit.

Out with the old.

In with the new.

I feel water all around me. Maybe I'm becoming one with all of the elements.

I only hope *fire* isn't the one that lasts for eternity.

When do I get to meet God?

Or do I?

Uh oh…

I feel a small hand slide into one of mine, and I clutch it. I'm not scared of bein' here in limbo. Back on earth, days of waitin' around in the Killjoy DMV to get my tickets settled seem to have really prepared me for this day. I give the hand a reassurin' squeeze.

"She's grabbing my hand!" The voice sounds like Dolly's. "She's alive! She's alive!"

"Maybe she has brain damage!" The voice sounds like Duncan.

Then, it sounds like Stokely says, "Coooooooool."

"Kids. Stop talking." It sounds like Isa again. Exasperated.

Another kiss. And firm pressure pulsin' hard through the center of me.

I have the sudden urge to sing "Staying Alive" by the Bee Gees in my head. *Oh the irony.* I'm dead and the only thing I want to karaoke is a song about stayin' alive! I just *knew* God had a sense of humor. She always seemed like she would.

Suddenly, I feel bad. Nauseous. Like I'm gon' barf everything I've ever eaten in seventy years.

I feel it spill out of me.

"Ewwwwww, she puked on you!" Duncan's voice again.

"Uma? Uma? Can you hear me?"

The voice sounds like an angel this time. A rugged stuntman turned seraphim.

Cosmo Goodman.

Another kiss. And then,

My vision returns. The blackness fades. I'm discombobulated.

Cosmo's lips pull away from mine, and I erupt like a broken fountain, spewin' water right onto the salt-and-pepper hair of his sternum.

I hear overjoyed cheers, and my head bobbles from side to side to take in my surroundings. It feels like everyone I know is kneelin' around me. Jagged limestone rock digs into my back. A wicked headache hits me like a freight train.

I don't think I'm dead at all.

I'm on the first platform in the *cenote*.

I'm alive.

…And I've just yacked water full of God-knows-what onto the most attractive man I know. If I weren't in so much pain, I'd be so embarrassed that I'd slip back into that blue water and finish the job.

I start to sit up.

"No," Cosmo says, tryin' to push me back down. "You could have injuries. A broken neck or spinal fracture."

But all I can think about is Cooper, and not lettin' the man get away with one, almost two, murders.

"Let me be." I sound crankier than I ought to be. After all, Cosmo just saved my life, and I'm surrounded by friends and family. I look down at my hand, and Dolly is holding it, tears streamin' down her perfect little face.

"I… I thought you died," she sobs. Then, she lunges at me, buryin' her head in my rib cage and enveloping me with her scrawny little arms.

Isa is fighting back tears. Duncan stands up, lookin' really bummed that I survived. Cosmo is starin' at me with a relieved smile and big glacier-blue eyes. He leans in and plants a kiss on my forehead.

"We have to stop Cooper!" I say as I pull away, my mission to stop him renewed.

"No need, Uma. Beat you to it," Devin shouts from twenty feet away on the same low rock platform he was before. I follow his voice with my eyes, and I see Cooper there, sittin' on his butt, soaked to the bone, a tendril of blood runnin' down his forehead. He glares at me and struggles, confined at the wrists by what looks like the drawstring of Devin's swim trunks, judgin' by how much of his pale butt crack is showin' now.

Cooper mutters a string of expletives at me, and then I hear a splash. I whip my head over to look at the source of it.

"Found it!" Stokely is wearin' my bedazzled snorkel and goggles with all the pink rhinestones. He has Lawrence's water-logged phone in his hand.

Dolly smiles at me. "Uma, we got him."

29

Day 4 - *5:37 pm*
Luncheonette at Cenote Santa Rosa
Yucatan, Mexico

I take another bite of my soft taco and pound the dark wooden table with my closed fist. "That is so good. I think it's the *achiote* and the lime that really make it, you know?"

"The avocado is a nice touch, too," Isa says before polishin' off her third and final taco.

"Thank you for givin' me yours," I say to Cosmo.

He hoists a beer toward me like he's about to toast. "You earned it, Uma Mae."

"Mee-Maw, do you want my milk?" Stokely asks, makin' a horrid face. "I think it's gone bad."

"It's not milk. It's *horchata.* And yeah, I'll take it."

As Stokely slides it across the table, I see a pair of Mexican police escort Cooper Nagilnick past the windowless restaurant, limping. He glares at me with hate-filled eyes.

Dolly sees him do it. "I just hope he never gets out, Uma. You might have a *Dead Calm* situation on your hands."

"You really gotta start watchin' more age-appropriate stuff, Dolly."

A live band starts playin' traditional music, and a woman in a white dress and a tight bun of dark hair with flowers in it steps out into the aisle between the tables. A young man in an all-white suit and a hat joins her. He's dressed like Michael Jackson sans jewel-encrusted white glove. They dance. Everyone who isn't eatin' claps at the spectacle.

After the song, the band plays another, and the couple starts pullin' people out of their chairs and encouraging them to dance. Before they reach our table, Cosmo stands and holds his hand out.

"Dance with me, Uma Mae."

Duncan makes a big deal out of it with a "Ooooooooooh," like he's about to start chantin' the K-I-S-S-I-N-G song on the playground. I ignore him.

"When in Rome, I suppose," I say, rising from my seat.

"Actually, this is the Yucatan," Stokely says, never able to fully comprehend a joke.

Cosmo holds my hand and slides his other to my mid back, glidin' us around the aisle to the beat.

"I really owe you one, Mr. Goodman. You saved my life today."

Cosmo blushes a little and looks away. "Just happy you didn't die. That was such a high fall. You could have broken your neck."

"I really thought I had. Pretty sure I used that hobbit to break my fall. Or soften the impact or whatever."

"I wouldn't have agreed to do that fall for all the money in Hollywood. You're an impressive woman."

I laugh. "Maybe I could have a lucrative career in stunts, too. We should see how well I bounce off the hood of a speedin' Benz next."

He chuckles softly, dodgin' us around another pair of cruise-goers dancin' their dinners off. "Let's maybe not do that, Uma Mae."

We sway a little more. Finally, I get the nerve up to say, "You know, of all the times I thought about kissin' you, I never once actually pictured it bein' durin' CPR."

After a pause, he replies, "Mmm. So you are sayin' you thought about kissin' me… More than once?" He's full-on blushin' now.

I shrug. "Yeah. It's crossed my mind a time or two. But the thought never included me upchuckin' dirty cave water in your face right afterward."

He laughs and spins me. He brings me back in tight to his body. "Well, then, maybe sometime when we're back in Killjoy, and there aren't so many people around, we can have ourselves a do-over."

Now, *I'm* the one blushin'.

"Well… I'd certainly be amenable to that." I try to fight my smile. "'Specially when my breath doesn't reek of *horchata* and *achiote*."

"Well, then," he presses his cheek to mine and whispers in my ear, *"it's a date."*

30

Day 5 - *11:45 am*
Minnow Pool
Lido Deck

"Here, Isa, hold my boba for a second. Everyone squeeze in real tight. That sun is in my eyes, and I can't really see too well. I wanna try to get Nawlins all in the background of this-here group photo," I say, hoistin' my phone up high into the air on my new selfie stick. I broke down and bought one at Jenny's kiosk, just so I could see what all the fuss was about.

You know... YOLO, as Stokely always says.

"Everyone in?" I ask the gaggle of people behind me. Devin gives me a thumbs up. Dolly hugs my waist. Duncan and Stokely are busy spittin' off the side of the boat, tryin' to hit the people below. Daniel and Jane look equally hungover in matchin' black wayfarers, *the lightweights.* Cosmo and Isa squeeze in beside me.

"Is this everybody?"

"Ma, just take the picture," Daniel groans.

"Alright, on the count of three, everyone say '*Laissez les bons temps rouler!*' One… Two… Three!"

Everyone around me just says "Cheese" in unison. I press the button on the stick and hold it.

"Okay, either I got one, or I got a hundred. We'll see later." I pop the phone off, and the wad of people loosens. "Well, y'all, it has been a *real* trip."

"A vacation I will not soon forget," Devin announces.

"It was nice meetin' you. Thanks for throwin' that flask. I'm sorry the kids never found it down there in the *cenote*," I say, leanin' in close.

He smiles at me. "It's for the best. I think that's gonna be my last drink. Like, *ever*."

"Well, whatever happened in your past, you saved me. I hope that restores some balance and peace, kid."

He hugs me, and I allow it.

Barely.

As Devin walks away, I try to kneel down to get on Dolly's level. When my ankle pops, I think better of it and decide to stay standin'. I reach into my purse.

"I got somethin' for you. A little trinket to remember me by." I hand her a folder bearing the Aspire logo.

She smiles and opens it. She looks like she is going to cry when she realizes it's the photo that Jenny took of us about four minutes before the more *morbid* part of our journey together began. She is posed like one of Charlie's

Angels. I've got my arms crossed like the cranky old codger I am. She flips it over and looks at the back, where I have written a message for her that says:

Stop watching so many adult movies and be a kid, for God's sake. Keep in touch.
Text, though. Don't ever call.
-Uma Blanchard

My scribbled signature is followed by my cell number. Dolly clutches it to her chest and starts to walk away, tears welling in her eyes. "You're gonna regret ever giving me your number."

"Oh, trust me, I already do," I say with a grin. I think she knows my insult is really code for, *I'm gonna miss you, twerp.*

As Dolly walks away huggin' her overpriced photo, Cosmo says into my ear, "That was a nice thing you done."

"She's an alright kid." I smile and look at my watch. *Ugh, time to start the sluggish disembarkation process.*

"You think you're done gettin' into trouble for a while?" Cosmo looks out at the water and then at me.

I can't help but laugh. "Oh, absolutely not."

"I didn't suspect you were." Cosmo holds out a bent arm for me. "Shall we?"

"We shall," I say as I take it.

ABOUT THE AUTHOR

Trixie is an award-winning author and filmmaker, an artist, a film industry grip, and a cancer survivor. Born in Wyoming, she spent most of her adult life in central Florida and southern Louisiana. She now lives on the beach in Connecticut.

When she isn't writing or reading, she is tending her massive vegetable garden, solving cold case files with her younger sister, singing her heart out at karaoke, or kayak fishing.

Trixie Fairdale is a cozy mystery pen name (an easy way to keep her various genre fiction separate for readers.) She has also published award-winning horror and fantasy under her real name, Erica Summers. She also writes contemporary romance under the pen name Odessa Alba.

AN UMA BLANCHARD COZY MYSTERY
TRIXIE FAIRDALE
LARGE PRINT EDITION!
MOURNING WAFFLES
BOOK ONE

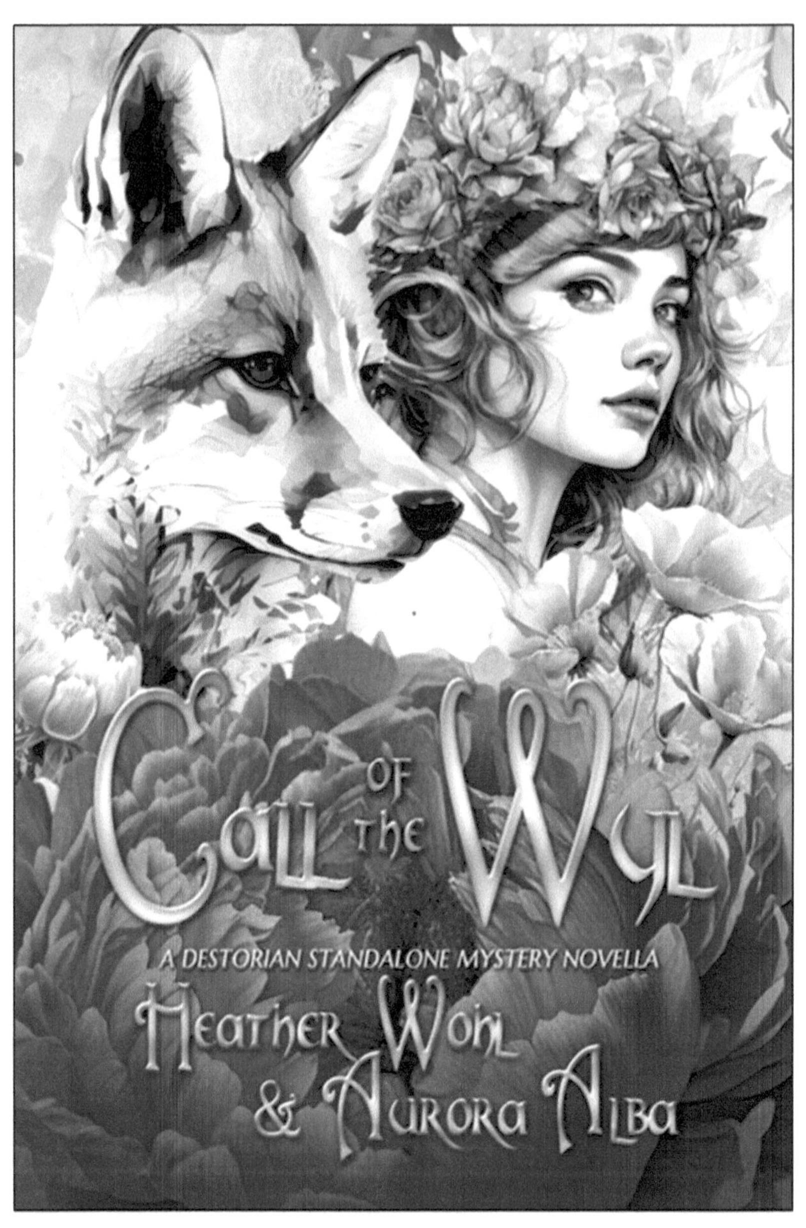

Call
of the Wyl
A DESTORIAN STANDALONE MYSTERY NOVELLA
Heather Wohl
& Aurora Alba

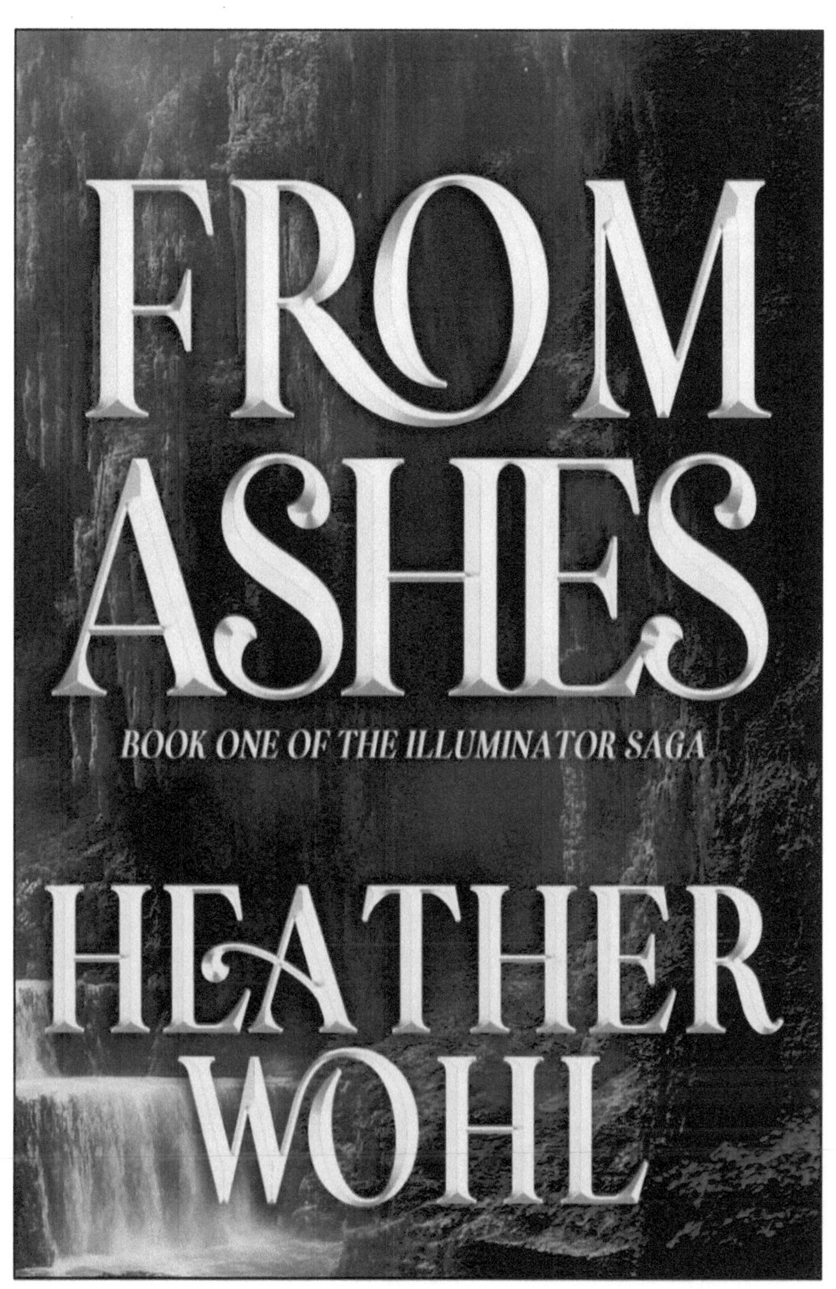

FROM ASHES
BOOK ONE OF THE ILLUMINATOR SAGA
HEATHER WOHL

The
Great Timbers
PENCRAFT AWARDS
A BEST BOOK
WINNER
WINTER 2024
LITERARY EXCELLENCE
James A. Kane

SIZE
DOESN'T
MATTER
A BEGINNER'S GUIDE TO MAXIMIZING
SMALL GARDEN SPACES FOR BIG HARVESTS
ERICA SUMMERS

The
Ugly
Sweater
PARTY
a Holidate Romance Novel
AURORA ALBA
& ODESSA ALBA